T.M. CROMER

Boundless Magic Copyright © 2024 T.M. Cromer
All rights reserved.

ISBN: 978-1-956941-26-5 (ebook)
ISBN: 978-1-956941-48-7 (paperback)

No part of this book may be reproduced in any form or by any electronic or mechanical means, including information storage and retrieval systems, without written permission from the author, except for the use of brief quotations in a book review.

This is a work of fiction. Names, characters, businesses, places, events and incidents are either the products of the author's imagination or used in a fictitious manner. Any resemblance to actual persons, living or dead, or actual events is purely coincidental.

NO AI TRAINING: Without in any way limiting the author's [and publisher's] exclusive rights under copyright, any use of this publication to "train" generative artificial intelligence (AI) technologies to generate text is expressly prohibited. The author reserves all rights to license uses of this work for generative AI training and development of machine learning language models.

Cover Design: Deranged Doctor Designs
Editor: Trusted Accomplice

AVAILABLE FROM T.M. CROMER

Get your printable list here:
www.tmcromer.com/printable-booklist

PARANORMAL ROMANCE

The Sentinels of Magic Series:
THE AETHER
THE DEATH DEALER
THE SEER

The Unlucky Charms Series:
PINTS & POTIONS
WHISKEY & WITCHES
BEER & BROOMSTICKS
COCKTAILS & CAULDRONS
WINE & WARLOCKS
HIGHBALLS & HEXES

The Thorne Witches Series:
SUMMER MAGIC
AUTUMN MAGIC
WINTER MAGIC
SPRING MAGIC

REKINDLED MAGIC

LONG LOST MAGIC

FOREVER MAGIC

ESSENTIAL MAGIC

MOONLIT MAGIC

ENCHANTED MAGIC

CELESTIAL MAGIC

EVERLASTING MAGIC

CAPTIVATING MAGIC

The Thorne Witches: Happily Ever Afters Series:

ENDURING MAGIC

BOUNDLESS MAGIC

The Angels of Legend Series:

LUCIFER

GABRIEL

CONTEMPORARY & ROMANTIC SUSPENSE

The Fiore Vineyard Series:

PICTURE THIS

RETURN HOME

ONE WISH

The Holt Family Series:

GOODBYE TO YOU

THIS TIME YOU
INCLUDING YOU
A LIFE WITH YOU

The Stonebrooke Series:
BURNING RESOLUTION
HIDDEN RESOLUTION

1

"**C**hloe's missing!"

Autumn froze in her tracks to stare at Keaton, and the door slammed shut behind her as if to emphasize her husband's panic-stricken declaration. "What do you mean she's missing? How long, and what about Jolly? She was supposed to be watching him."

Keaton's normally tanned face paled. The contrast was so dramatic, Autumn's heart stalled before kicking into overdrive.

"Tell me you checked on Jolly." There wasn't exactly a threat in her tone, but a mere mortal would probably have wet their pants when they heard the outrage in her voice.

They both raced for the playroom, with Keaton beating her by a mere foot. After skidding to a halt just inside the door, her heart dropped through the floor as her adrenaline spiked.

It was empty.

"I'll check his room. You call the rest of your family."

"Jesus, Autumn. It was fifteen minutes. I'll never forgive—"

"Recriminations later, babe. We have kids to find."

After a thorough search of her son's room turned up empty, Autumn ran to the ceremony chamber in the basement, and with a wave of her hand, the candles around the circle flared to life. Upstairs, she could hear Keaton thudding around, and it seemed he was everywhere at once, searching for the kids. His shouts grew faint, and she could only assume he'd run outside to check there.

With grim determination, she dragged a scrying mirror to the pentagram's center and sat cross-legged on the floor. She removed the "Keaton for Mayor" election pin from her suit jacket and looked at it. Her husband's handsome face, with his enchanting grin and dancing aquamarine eyes, stared back at her. As usual, his shaggy, dark hair had fallen over one brow prior to the picture being taken, making him appear like a rakish billionaire out to seduce innocents. Yet he had a trustworthy quality that shone through and made people instinctively gravitate toward him. He'd be the next mayor, without question.

Centering herself with a few deep, cleansing breaths, Autumn used the back of the pin to stab her index finger and squeeze exactly three drops of blood onto the mirror for a tried-and-true spell. If she could find Jolyon, chances were Chloe would be with him.

"Goddess, hear my plea.
Assist me in this time of need.
Use this blood and reveal to me,
blood of my blood, the child I seek."

The purplish-red droplets merged into one and turned black, dissolving into a puff of smoke. When the haze lifted and Autumn could see into the glass, Jolly's laughing face, almost identical to her husband's, shone back at her. Tears blurred her vision before she hastily blinked them away.

"Where are you, my little man?" she whispered.

The image shifted, and Autumn could see Chloe tearing through the woods as if being chased by the demons of hell. Her cheeks were tear streaked, and her dark hair was a rat's nest with twigs and leaves tangled throughout. Chloe was frantic, and if Autumn didn't miss her guess, she was searching for her little brother.

"Show me Jolyon," she commanded the mirror.

Again, he laughed, and this time, he was clapping his hands with joy.

"Who is he with?"

But the blood on the mirror fizzled to nothing, and the image disappeared from view. Terror tried to take hold and clog her throat.

Autumn jumped to her feet and bolted up the basement steps to the main floor, screaming Keaton's name. At the top of the stairs, she was greeted by Spring and Knox.

"Keaton texted and asked if we could come right over. The kids are missing?" Spring's jade-green eyes were filled with concern.

"Yes! Scrying only shows me Chloe's location. Jolly's comes up blank." Autumn felt as if her skin was too tight, too itchy, too everything. She needed to find her children—like yesterday!

"I'm scared, sister," she confessed. "I've never been so scared."

Knox drew her into his comforting arms and kissed the top of her head. "Hold it together a little longer, and tell me where you saw Chloe. I'll go."

"Running through the woods, and if I had to guess, it would be the section dividing this property from Thorne Manor. Close to the glen." As he turned to go, she gripped his arm. "She looked terrified, Knox."

He nodded and shot a speaking glance at Spring. "Stay here, and find a way to locate Jolyon. If anyone can do it, it's you."

"I'm going with you, cousin," Keaton said from behind them.

"I'll find her faster alone. Help Autumn and Spring."

"She's my fucking daughter!"

"I love her, too, Keat. And you can be damned sure I'll kill anyone who might even think to hurt her." Knox gripped Keaton's shoulder and shook it gently. "I've got this, and Autumn needs you."

With blazing speed, Knox teleported away.

"Come on, Tums," Spring said. "Show me what you've tried to locate Jolly."

They jogged downstairs and entered the ceremony room with Keaton on their heels.

Autumn explained the spell and what she'd seen. "The image doesn't show anything in the background. It's impossible to tell where he is."

"What if we added my blood and magic to the mix, along with Spring's?" Keaton asked.

Having only recently come into his abilities, he didn't have the vast knowledge of her Thorne sisters, but he was willing to try whatever they might suggest if it meant bringing his son home in one piece. For that alone, Autumn adored him.

"Tell me what to do, babe," he said, gripping her hand.

"You should know, if he's been taken, it depends on how powerful the witch is who holds him," Spring said grimly. "I'm not saying that's what happened, but it's better to prepare yourself for action."

"I agree it's a possibility," Autumn said. "I can't see Chloe wandering off with Jolly in tow. She's too responsible."

"Where's the Carlyle grimoire, sissy?"

Although she had a photographic memory, Spring always liked to double-check before performing a spell. Hands down, she was the most skilled of Autumn's sisters, but it could be argued that Summer and Winnie were the most powerful.

"I'm still at a loss how anyone got past our wards. Only the Aether has the power to take them down." Autumn doused the candles and paced the room, unable to remain still while Spring selected a spell. "I thought all our enemies were neutralized. How the fuck is this happening?"

"I'm sorry, babe," Keaton said, his voice achingly sweet and full of regret. "I'm so sorry. I shouldn't have left Chloe to watch him."

Although she was holding on to her sanity by a fraying thread, she couldn't let her husband shoulder the blame. She wrapped her arms around his neck and buried her face against his throat, sighing when his arms tightened around her.

"It's not your fault, Keaton. We both believed Chloe was up to the task of watching him for short bursts of time. You couldn't predict you'd be needed in the barn —" She jerked away and stared. "Wait! What was wrong with the horse? Was it a sudden onset?"

Horror dawned on her husband's already ragged

face, but it quickly dissipated, and he shook his head. "No. I'm positive it was typical founder. Unless someone was watching us for months on end, there's no way anyone could've staged this. They wouldn't have had the opportunity before now."

2

Keaton's gut clenched at the initial conclusion Autumn had drawn. He'd had to really give it some thought to determine if the incident in the barn was connected. But no. It couldn't have been. Their horse Lazy Jay was prone to founder, and nothing about his current condition led Keaton to believe it was anything but bad luck and bad timing. Yet his kids were missing, and it was his damned fault for not calling one of his or his wife's family members to come babysit.

Chloe had seemed so confident that she could take care of her toddler brother for a short time, and Keaton hadn't wanted to hurt her feelings by denying she could. She'd sworn she wanted the responsibility, and at age twelve, she should've been able to care for Jolyon for a few hours, much less fifteen minutes.

All Keaton knew was that he'd never forgive

himself if harm came to either of them. Neither would Autumn, despite how understanding and self-contained she was at the moment.

His gaze met and held Spring's, and behind her bright eyes, he could see the wheels turning in her clever mind. The woman's IQ was off the charts, and there wasn't a situation she couldn't resolve, given enough time.

"What are you thinking?" he asked.

"You said this wasn't staged, and I tend to agree. But I can't for the life of me figure out how they could simply disappear on their own. It makes no sense that Tums would see Chloe running from someone." Spring flicked her thick chestnut hair over her shoulder in an absent gesture and strode over to the altar that contained the Carlyle grimoire and another, bigger book. She pointed to the one he'd never seen before. "Is this book always left out?"

Keaton met Autumn's amber eyes and shared a confused look. "No. Didn't you pull it out when you performed your scrying spell, babe?"

She shook her head, and her rich auburn hair tumbled from its updo. "Actually, no. I used a spell I remembered from the Thorne book." His wife joined her sister by the altar. She paled when she read the selected page. "I don't think anyone took our children, Keaton. I think they teleported themselves to another dimension."

"What?" His heart stalled inside his chest, then

kicked back in at double time. "Another dimension? Please tell me you're joking."

"She's not," Spring replied grimly. "There are traces of unrefined magic in the air. A novice performed this spell without a circle. Can you feel it too, Tums?"

Nodding, Autumn compressed her lips in a tight, white line. "Chloe should've known better. We've been teaching her how to practice since she was eight."

"It'll be all right, sissy. I promise," Spring said with a quick, hard hug. "We need to call Knox back. I don't think he's going to find the children in the woods. Or at least not the ones on this plane. That could also be why Chloe was terrified in your vision, Tums."

"Right. Because she couldn't get back to the house!"

"Christ! What does that mean for them? Where the hell could she have taken Jolly?" Sweat broke out on Keaton's lower back, and his hands grew clammy as his gut churned. "And why? Why would she take him there without permission?"

The sisters shared a worried glance, and it didn't serve to make him any less stressed.

"What the fuck lives in the dimension they're in?" he asked. "Is it possible our enemies exist there?"

"In answer to your first question, I don't know. To the second, maybe. I'd like to say it's a simple yes or no response," Spring replied. "But I'm not going to play the candyman and sugarcoat my answers. I'm sorry, Keaton. This entire situation is a little more complicated than that."

"How?"

"First, we need to see if we can communicate across the divide. Once we can get a better idea of what's going on, we can find a way to get them back."

As her sister spoke, Autumn returned to his side and placed a calming hand over his heart. Although he recognized she was as frightened as him, she also had more experience in a crisis and was holding onto her cool better than he ever could.

"Keaton, please go upstairs and find Knox, then your parents. We need to know whatever Keira and Phillip might about this spell. I'm going to assist Spring in locating a communication spell. If we can figure out what Chloe did and why, it might help us."

"What if we can't locate them or, Goddess forbid, get them back?" he demanded. "Can one of us be sent there?"

His wife's expression hardened. "You can bet on it. I'm not leaving our children in an alternate dimension. But we're not one hundred percent positive that happened yet."

The longer he delayed, the more chance they had of failing, but Keaton couldn't seem to make his feet walk up those steps. His need to be more proactive in retrieving his kids was causing a strange paralysis he couldn't seem to overcome.

Meeting Autumn's challenging stare, he nodded.

Trust.

It was an important factor in any marriage, and

they shared that. Every now and again, he had to let go and allow his wife to do what she felt was necessary. Usually, her way was the right way, but old habits died hard, and his protectiveness of Chloe was the oldest habit he had.

"Babe?"

"I'm going," he said gruffly. Hauling Autumn close, he absorbed the comfort he needed but could never request aloud. "Thank you for loving Chloe as much as you do."

"She's our daughter," Autumn replied. To her, it was simple. Chloe was as much hers as Jolly, whether she was her natural parent or not. "Thornes don't know how to fail, babe."

Because she was right, Keaton grinned despite his overwhelming fear. "That's what I'm counting on."

3

As soon as her husband was gone, Autumn addressed her sister. "How bad is it if they jumped realities?"

"Scale of one to ten?"

Swallowing back her panic, she nodded.

Spring's grimace screamed, "Fifteen."

"Okay. No need to say it." Pressing her palm to her forehead, Autumn sighed and looked down at the ancient tome. "How do we reverse engineer the spell the kids used so we can return home once we've found them?"

"That's a bit trickier, I believe. Not only that, but we're going to need permission from Isis to jump alternate planes. This isn't a run-of-the-mill situation. I don't know what happens when or if we meet our counterparts. It could create a cosmic shitstorm."

"There's a possibility of that?"

"It's all supposition, Tums. Other than a trip to the Netherworld, I've never done anything like this."

Dropping her hand, she nodded. "All right. I'll leave you to read this book, since you're the one with the photographic memory. I'll see about summoning the Goddess for permission after I shoot a text to Dad and Uncle Alastair."

"Good idea. If anyone has any experience with this, it's them. Dad might have some good insight since he resided in the Otherworld so long." Spring smiled prettily as she always did when she had a solid plan of attack.

"I hadn't thought of that, but you're right," Autumn said, returning her smile. "If Isis answers anyone's call, it will be his or Uncle Alastair's."

As she turned to go, Spring caught her arm.

"We'll get them back, Tums. I promise you I won't rest until I do."

Overcome with gratitude and love, she hugged her youngest sister tightly. "You really are the family jewel, sissy. You are forever bright, beautiful, and kind. We are so blessed to have you in our lives."

"I say that every single day," Knox said from somewhere behind Autumn. His voice was packed with adoration for the woman he loved enough to fight the world and the heavens for.

A becoming blush tinged Spring's cheeks as she met her mate's gaze. Theirs were two souls that had survived many incarnations and would always find the other, regardless of time and circumstance. They were two halves of the same whole, and a couple more devoted to each other would be difficult to find.

"And so you should," Autumn replied with an arched brow. "She's da bomb."

"True. She blew up my world in the best possible way," he responded with a wide grin.

"Pfft. That was corny as hell."

"You started with the cheesy phrases. Now go calm your husband as I kiss my bright, beautiful, and kind woman."

Knox closed the distance and wrapped a large hand around the back of Spring's neck, gently tangling his fingers in her hair. The look of love he graced her with was heart melting to anyone observing. No one could witness his emotion for her and not be awed by it.

"Don't distract her. She has to help me find my kids," Autumn warned. "Time is of the essence here."

With a quick press of his lips to Spring's, Knox released her. "We know, and we're going to get them back, Autumn. Count on it."

Tears stung her eyes, and she nodded. "Thank you. Both of you!"

After blinking away the moisture, Autumn dashed up the stairs and grabbed her cellphone from the counter. A shuffling in the children's playroom caught her attention, and she went to check it out.

Nothing.

Frowning at the large indentation on the daybed,

she started toward it, then stopped, mentally waving off the oddity. It was a mystery for another day. Right now, she had to get her father here. Deciding a call was better than a text, she dialed his number.

"Autumn? What's wrong, honey?"

"The kids are missing, Daddy," she croaked out. What was it about her father's confidant voice that turned her into a small child again?

"Missing?"

Before she could reply, the connection dropped and there was a pounding on the front door. She rushed to the foyer.

Preston Thorne, her personal superhero, didn't bother waiting for an answer and, instead, shoved open the door and entered the foyer. When his worried amber gaze locked with hers, he opened his arms, inviting her for a comforting hug.

Autumn flew across the room and dove into his embrace.

"Tell me what's happening, sweetheart."

"We don't know much other than we think they teleported to an alternate dimension. Spring and I were hoping you and Uncle Alastair could help us."

"Of course. Have you already come up with an action plan?"

"Spring and Knox are down in the ceremony room, studying the book we think Chloe may have used. Keaton is checking with his parents to see what they know, if anything, about it." She drew back and ran shaky fingers under her eyes to hide the tears that escaped. "It's dusty as hell and looks to be older than this house."

"Okay. Call Al while I go down and look at the book. If Keira and Phillip come back, direct them to us." Her father tilted her chin up. Giving her a warm smile, he said, "They'll be home by suppertime."

"Have you had experience with your kids teleporting to an alternate plane, Dad? If not, I'm going to call bullshit on your overconfidence."

He chuckled, and Autumn could hear the tension he tried to hide.

"Go on. See what Spring's found," she said with a sigh. "I'll call Uncle Alastair and see if maybe he can contact Isis to request permission for the spell."

"Good idea." With a kiss to her forehead, he shifted to go. He hadn't moved more than two steps before he turned back. "The *Book of Thoth*. I remember seeing it in Isis's keeping. Ask if she will allow us to borrow the portal spell from it."

Spring entered the room with Knox on her heels. She waved the tome in the air and grinned. "No need. From what I can tell, this is almost an exact replica of the *Book of Thoth*."

No one needed to ask how she knew it was the same. Spring had already read the original, and her photographic memory could verify if what they had was a duplicate.

"That's not good," Autumn muttered. "That fucking thing has been nothing but trouble, if you ask me."

"True. Especially the spells opening portals," Knox added. "Considering an exchange always has to be made, I'm wondering what came through to this side and how we find it."

4

"Is that a real possibility?" Autumn asked. Her horror at her children accidentally unleashing some monstrous creature on the unsuspecting citizens of Leiper's Fork made her stomach drop ten feet below ground.

"A possibility, yes. You should be asking if it's along the lines of a probability, though." Knox grimaced. "The answer is also yes."

She shared a concerned look with her father before saying, "Okay. We'll wait for the fallout in case it's some Godzilla creature, but for now, we need to find my kids."

"We should still seek permission for using any of the spells from this book, Autumn." Preston's expression was heart-attack serious. They all knew the backlash involved in defying a goddess.

"I know, Dad. I intend to. The three of you work

out what we need for this. I'm going to the clearing to summon Uncle Alastair and, with him, Isis."

She stepped out the back door, closing it behind her. As she dialed her uncle, her gaze fell on the barn in the distance and, behind that building, the woods where she and Keaton used to meet when they first fell in love. So much had happened in that time. So many years filled with heartache, then eventually, love.

Autumn walked in that direction just as Alastair answered the call.

"We need you, Uncle," she said without preamble. "Can you teleport to the clearing between my house and Thorne Manor?"

"I'll be there momentarily."

"Thank you."

"You never have to thank me, child. I know if you're calling, it's important."

Gratitude closed her throat, and she couldn't speak. But he didn't wait for her reply, and the line went dead.

With a searching study of her surroundings to ascertain no mortals were in the general vicinity, Autumn closed her eyes and visualized the glen where their family performed ceremonies. Her cells warmed to burning, but before it became unbearable, the wind kicked up. The cool breeze caressed her face, whipping her hair around her head and providing necessary relief.

Goddess, she loved the ability to teleport anywhere

in the world in seconds. There was a sense of freedom attached to the act. As if she could always escape the demands of life by visualizing where she wanted to go.

When she lifted her lids, Alastair was there, his hands raised to the sky. A half smile curled his lips as he watched her.

"Better?"

He referred to the cooling breeze he'd created, and Autumn appreciated his thoughtfulness.

"Much." She strode forward and hugged him tightly.

There had been a time when they were at odds due to misunderstandings, mostly on her part, but she'd come to adore her renegade uncle. Many times, his fuck-the-world-I'm-doing-it-anyway attitude had saved someone she loved, and Autumn could appreciate the hell out of his tactics.

"What's the problem, child?"

It was humorous that he would call a woman approaching forty "child," but from a warlock almost twice her age, it seemed fitting.

"My children have gone missing," she said simply.

All humor fell from him, and his classically handsome visage grew stony. "What do you mean? Has someone abducted them?"

"Not that we can tell, but we aren't sure. Spring believes Chloe may have transported herself and Jolly through a portal into another plane, using a spell from a duplicate *Book of Thoth*."

Alastair's skin took on a sickly cast. "Are you positive?"

"Not one hundred percent, but close. There's a magical signature attached to a page that was opened in the book."

"Christ!"

"My thought exactly." She touched his arm to keep his attention. "Dad's at the house with Spring and Knox. Keaton's trying to hunt down his parents to see what they know."

"But you've asked me here for another reason," he concluded.

"Yes. If my kids did, in fact, cross planes, we need to seek permission from Isis to open the portal to retrieve them. We also need to find who or what may have come through in exchange for their entry."

"I'll get my security team on capturing whoever or whatever is here, if anything. We'll need to return it to its own reality." Gripping her hand, he squeezed it lightly. "You and I will need to summon the Goddess."

"That's what I was hoping."

"Let's cast the protection circle. The last thing we need is to have something or someone attack while we are calling her forward."

"On it."

Together, they created a ring of candles, drawing sigils in the four directions: north, south, east, and west. Then, when they were satisfied, they joined hands.

Autumn spoke first.

"Goddess, hear our plea.
Assist us in our time of need."

"Exalted One, we call on you to help us find Autumn's children," Alastair added.

Ringing began in Autumn's ears, and the atmospheric change was electrifying. Frowning, she locked gazes with her uncle, startled to see his confusion.

Something was wrong.

"What is it—"

"Shh, child," he whispered.

Releasing her hands, he walked along the boundaries of the circle as if testing for weakness. His head cocked as he listened for Goddess knew what.

"It's as if she can't come through," he murmured, talking to himself.

A heavy frown tugged at his dark-blond brows, and the concern on his face ramped up Autumn's anxiety a hundredfold. Her heart felt like it was going to escape her chest and take flight. It was difficult to take a deep breath. How much of it was nerves, and how much was the weighty atmosphere? She couldn't say for certain, if questioned.

"What the fuck is happening?" she asked in a stage whisper.

"I—"

A feather could've knocked her over when Alastair's clone walked from the woods. Or rather, what he might've looked like if he ditched his tailored suits for flannel and let his hair and stubble grow unruly. Although he had a few scars on his face and neck and his sapphire eyes held the same alert expression as his counterpart, the guy appeared more down to earth. His rolling walk was relaxed despite his cautious expression.

"Holy hell! It's Paul-Bunyan Alastair!"

Other than a sharp glance, her uncle ignored Autumn to warily watch the other man approach. Clearly affronted that his clone would wear anything off the rack of the local farm store, Alastair was filled with disdain.

His arrogance was laughable.

The lumberjack version eyed them but never crossed the protective barrier. He seemed to take particular interest in her, making Autumn just as curious about him.

Stepping in front of her, Alastair drew the man's attention back to him. "Care to tell us who you are and why you're roaming these woods? This is private property."

"Lawd, tell me this version of me doesn't always walk around with a stick up his lily-white ass, Tums," Lumberjack Alastair said in a heavy Southern accent.

In an instinctive act, both she and her uncle clenched their fists to stem off the influx of locusts that came whenever Alastair swore. Better safe than sorry because who knew if the newcomer had the same curse?

"This version?" she asked, absently noting he sounded like Alastair's cousin Boyd.

Crossing his arms over his well-muscled chest, the clone snorted. "I wasn't born yesterday, girl. I knew immediately that I'd been thrust into another world. The question is, what the hell are y'all going to do about sending me back?"

They'd finally discovered what—or rather who—came through the portal her children had opened.

5

Isis was a no-show.

With Lumberjack Alastair waiting across the clearing, looking more bored than Autumn had ever seen the one from her time, she and her uncle closed the circle.

Keeping her voice low so it wouldn't carry, she asked, "What do we do about him? Do you think he's legit? Or is it possible he's someone glamoured to look like you?"

"I'm highly offended you believe that ruffian resembles me in any way," he replied with a sardonic smile.

Autumn paused to consider the earthier version of Alastair. "Oh, I don't know. He has a certain appeal for women."

"If he does, I'm not seeing it."

As her uncle tugged his cuffs and straightened his

tie, she struggled not to laugh. "Just don't let Rorie see him. She'll order you to dress in flannel shirts and hiking boots."

"Heaven forbid."

She laughed as he mock shuddered. When her uncle returned her grin with one of his own, Autumn knew he wasn't offended. "Should I get you a gift card for the local farm store? You might be able to find some Wranglers and a Stetson that fits."

"Your father didn't punish you enough as a child," Alastair muttered.

"He punished me plenty. I seem to recall *you* always snuck me out of my room to take me fishing."

His brows shot up. "You remember that?"

"Yeah. It was sweet. But don't for one second think I'm not aware you do it for the next generation."

His rare burst of laughter was robust, echoing off the surrounding trees and drawing the attention of Lumberjack Al. The other man straightened from his slouched position and headed in their direction.

"Do you think he's a decent guy just wanting to get home? I mean, he has the potential to be an evil asshat, right? Just like anyone, doesn't it depend on formative years?" she asked, rushing to get her concerns out while they were still alone.

"Yes." Alastair winked. "But he can't possibly be more formidable than your old uncle."

"That's what I'm hoping." She touched his arm.

"Let's get LJ and head home. I'm itchy and need to find my kids. They've been gone too long."

"LJ?" he asked as they strode across the glen.

"In my head, he's Lumberjack Alastair."

A quicksilver grin flashed, but he didn't comment.

As they reached his clone, the man gave them a bored look.

"Isis having none of it, girl?" he asked, choosing to ignore Uncle Alastair.

"Apparently. What do you know?"

"She's capricious at best. Little spitfire when riled—"

"Not of her! About this portal thing," she snapped.

"Same ol' Tums," he said with a smirk that Autumn wanted to slap off his face. "Impatient as always, aren't ya, girl?"

"My children are wandering around your world, unattended and probably scared out of their fucking minds, dude. So yeah, you can say I'm impatient."

LJ sobered and cast a fleeting glance at Alastair's stony countenance before addressing her. "Sorry, honey. Let's get to Thorne Manor and find a spell to reverse this, okay?"

"I don't live at Thorne Manor. The spell that was used was from the *Book of—*"

"It was from a book her husband's family possesses," Alastair cut in smoothly. Gesturing toward the path to the Carlyle estate, he said, "After you."

"If you're this uptight in your world, I wonder what my Angelica is like."

"Angelica?" Autumn and Alastair asked simultaneously.

"My wife."

She shared a look with her uncle, feeling like her surprise must've shot her brows right off her face. "Did you ever meet anyone named Angelica?"

With a frown and a shake of his head, he gave his rugged twin a small shove in the direction they were to walk.

"What the hell is this, then? Who did you marry, if not Angelica? Thornes only love once," LJ demanded with a scowl, refusing to budge an inch.

"Her name's Aurora Fennell. She's my mother," Autumn said despite her uncle's warning look. "Surely, you've met her?"

"Can't say I did, hon." LJ shrugged and moved toward her home.

"What about when you returned from the war?" she asked, somewhat desperately. If he'd never hooked up with her mother, two of her sisters were never born.

"Vietnam," Alastair added when the guy still appeared confused.

"No Vietnam war in my time," LJ replied with the standard Thorne shrug. If his appearance didn't already label him one of their own, his mannerisms certainly did.

His answer cleared up why he'd never met her mother in London, but it made no sense why he hadn't met her later, when she married Preston. If she even did. But she had to, right? Especially if there was a second Autumn.

Her head hurt from trying to figure it out.

"What about Preston?" Alastair asked the question she'd been wondering.

"My brother left home to backpack Europe after college. We didn't know about you girls until after word reached us that he and his wife died in that plane crash."

Autumn jerked to a halt. "Wait! What? What plane crash? Are you saying my parents are dead?"

Grief flashed briefly across LJ's visage. "I'm sorry, hon."

"But—"

"Let it go, child," Alastair said with surprising tenderness. "You'll only give yourself a headache, and there's no changing the past in his world."

She nodded and met LJ's sad sapphire eyes.

"I'm sorry for your loss," she said in a choked voice. Knowing her uncle could take care of himself, she bolted. Her need to find her children pounded through her with every step she ran. If she didn't get to them soon, she'd go insane.

6

Alastair walked beside his rough-and-ready counterpart from the alternate dimension, and the surreal nature of the moment wasn't lost on him.

No Rorie.

He shoved aside the urge to question his companion about Angelica and concentrated on the immediate—returning Jolly and Chloe to their rightful place and time. His primary concern was the fact Isis had not responded to his summons. Rarely did that happen unless she was irate over one of his misdeeds, which of late, had been none.

"I can feel ya thinking, Al," the guy said with a grimace. "It's like a fucking buzzing in my brain."

Alastair fisted his hand.

"Ya wanting to punch me?"

"Hardly. If I were to attack, it would be with magic.

I'm not likely to resort to barbaric brawls in the middle of the forest."

"Then what's with the fist?" LJ—*Dear Goddess! Was he really mentally calling the man that?*—paused his forward movement and gestured to Alastair's curled hand.

"In this world, I'm cursed. If I were to swear, it conjures an influx of pests."

The other man's guffaws were loud and oddly contagious, nothing like his own rusty laughter. "Are ya having me on, right now?"

"Deadly serious, I'm afraid. Would you care for me to swear and prove it?"

"Nah." Sobering, LJ began walking again. "I'll take your word for it." With a curious side glance, he asked, "What did you do to deserve it?"

"I ventured into the Otherworld without an invitation, then snuck back out."

"Why the hell would you do that?"

After a brief hesitation to listen for locusts and hearing none, Alastair said, "As you stated earlier, Thornes only love once. Rorie was there, and I intended to bring her home."

"Not Angelica," LJ stated flatly. "Did you ever meet her?"

"No," Alastair said. He had briefly known a woman named Angelica, but he wasn't positive they were discussing the same person. It was pointless to explain it was during his imprisonment. He'd experienced a fondness for the woman, but she'd died because he'd made the mistake of casting her a reassuring smile in the presence of his greatest enemies, Zhu Lin and Victor Salinger. Instead, Alastair would silently carry the guilt to his grave with the rest of his sins.

"You're lying."

Surprised, he jerked to a halt. Meeting his own assessing gaze was disturbing on multiple levels, and a fire burned behind LJ's stare. The man was angry about his falsehood.

"I didn't want to cause you unnecessary hurt," Alastair stated coolly. Going with the assumption that both women were the same, he said, "Angelica never survived the Witches' War. I'm sorry."

The man sucked in a breath, and perhaps it would've been better had Alastair punched him in the face, because LJ's shock was great, as was the wave of angst coming from him.

"Please, rein your emotions in," Alastair gritted out. Finally, he had an idea of the pain others received whenever he lost control of his anger.

"Sorry. I just…" Shaking his head, LJ stalked off in Autumn's wake.

As Alastair strolled at a more sedate pace, keeping his twin in sight, he played the problem over in his mind. The only reason Isis wouldn't respond was because she couldn't. Somehow, the children had caused a cosmic shift. If it wasn't righted soon, chaos would ensue.

With a dark frown pulling at his brows, LJ stormed back to him. "I think those kids of Tums caused a cosmic shift."

A bark of laughter escaped Alastair.

"What's so goddamned funny?"

"I'd just come to that exact conclusion."

"Hmm. Well, what can I say? We're practically the same person." He eyed Alastair's suit. "Or we would be if you weren't such a tight ass. Why are you?"

"I abhor dirt of any kind." When LJ's dark blond brows shot up, Alastair elaborated. "I was held prisoner for a number of years, bound by magical shackles and living in my own filth. No clean water for drinking or bathing to be had. Only given enough food to keep me alive so I could be tortured daily."

Compassion came and went on the other man's face, as if he tried to hide it because he knew it wasn't welcome. "Makes sense. Let's go save Tums's kids."

"Tell me. In your world, does Autumn marry Keaton Carlyle?"

"Yeah. He's pretty much a worthless asshole. I don't understand what that girl sees in him. Never amounted to much."

"Really?" A grin curled Alastair's mouth. "You're in for a treat."

"You say that like he's something here."

"I can see we share the same powers of observation."

LJ chuckled. The man sobered and shot a side

glance his way. "You and Aurora Fennell, huh? What about Preston?"

"My brother never toured Europe out of school. The Witches' War was in progress when he was that age. Prior to that, I fought in a human war, then traveled to Europe to shuck the weight of what I'd seen." He shrugged. "I suppose you could say I needed a palate cleanser. My first day there, I saw Rorie reading a book at a small cafe and lost my heart."

"But you met Angelica during the Witches' War. When was that, and how did Aurora come to have children with your brother?" LJ met Alastair's inquiring gaze and smiled wryly. "The girl looks just like him, and she asked if her parents were dead."

"It's quite a long story, and if we have time, I'll fill you in on the details. However, right now, we've arrived at our destination." Alastair nodded toward the house as it came into view. "You'll find our brother through those double doors."

"Pres is here?"

"This version of him, yes."

His alternate-plane twin inhaled deeply, nodded once, and moved toward the patio. As LJ strode away, Alastair turned over their meeting in his mind. This crush of exchanged information was likely the reason they shouldn't reside in the same time and place. At any given moment, one or the other might be inclined to alter the other's fate by doing something to save a loved one or friend. With any luck, they'd get the children home and Lumberjack Al back to his proper world in a timely manner.

Alastair was just about to the pool deck when a shiny object caught his attention. He didn't swear aloud, but he sure as hell wanted to when he recognized the significance of the jewelry piece at his feet.

7

*A*utumn was in the middle of explaining about their portal visitor to the others when LJ walked into the room.

A hush fell over the small crowd.

"Holy crap!" Spring approached the man with avid curiosity on her lovely face.

In response, LJ scowled like he'd seen his worst enemy and backed up a step. Directing his question toward Autumn, he kept his wary gaze on her sister. "What's this, then? She's welcome here?"

"Welcome?" Perfectly arched chestnut brows shot up as Spring tilted her head to study LJ. "Am I not welcome where you come from?"

His distrust could be felt like crawly bugs along Autumn's arms, and curiosity got the better of her. Leaving her father's side, she crossed to him.

"She's the best of us in this world, LJ. But what has she done to you?"

"We'll just say she's not a nice person and leave it at that," he muttered.

Skirting her, he approached Preston. Sadness clouded his visage, and he appeared to be holding back his grief as he struggled with the idea of embracing his brother's twin. Autumn felt a twinge of sympathy for what he'd lost. The Thornes in this world had once experienced a similar emotion when her father crossed to the Otherworld for a time.

"Preston," he said gruffly. "You look the same."

One of her father's dark auburn brows lifted as he studied the rougher duplicate of his brother. "I can't say the same for you. Alternate Alastair, I'm assuming?"

"Lumberjack Al seems to work with all the flannel," Autumn said with a gesture toward his shirt.

LJ's grin was pure sunshine. "But I'm the better looking of the two."

"Debatable," Uncle Alastair said as he shut the glass doors. "However, we don't have time for this nonsense." Holding up Jolly's gift from the Goddess, he scowled. "We have an untethered Jolyon on the loose."

"Ohmygod!" Autumn felt faint. The anklet had been designed to contain her son's unimaginable power. There was no telling what havoc he could wreak in the world he currently inhabited.

"We have to get through that portal. Like *now*!"

Knox, who had been silent until then, stepped forward. "If he was strong enough to cause earthquakes as a baby, he's strong enough to—"

"Open a portal," Alastair added grimly. "Perhaps young Chloe isn't the culprit, after all."

Autumn's knees gave out, but Knox was there to catch her. "I have to tell Keaton."

"I'll do it. You sit down and process this for a minute," he said gently. "We'll get them back, Autumn. I promise."

"You can't promise that, Knox. You know you can't."

"I have a few tricks in my back pocket and a few people who owe me favors," he assured her. She didn't miss the concerned look he exchanged with her uncle and father.

"I'm not weak, nor am I unaware, fellas." She glared at the men around her. "I know how to read a damned room."

Admiration flared in her uncle's sapphire eyes, and he nodded his approval. "Keep that spirit, child. You're going to need it." Addressing Spring, he asked, "What do you remember of the ceremony to resurrect your mother, my dear?"

"All of it."

"Do we still have the artifacts in safekeeping?"

"I do. I'm assuming my sisters do as well," Spring said with a questioning glance at Autumn.

"No. The Chintamani Stone was put in the vault at

Thorne Industries for safekeeping, so were a few of the other items. But even if we still had all the key elements we needed, we no longer have the numbers to perform the ceremony."

As she was speaking, Keaton and his parents entered the room. Because he'd heard the tail end of her comment, he voiced his opinion. "Actually, I think we do, if you're talking about the spell that revived Aurora. From what I recall, there had to be seven blood relatives of your mother. Jolly has that with both our sides combined."

"Then it could work?" Autumn asked, scared to hope but feeling that small kernel of emotion ready to pop inside.

Her father shared a look with Alastair and LJ before nodding. "I think so. Remember, this isn't like opening the portal to the Otherworld, honey. We're opening it to another reality. There's no telling what the long-term consequences might be."

"They have to be better than my juiced-up kid running around unsupervised, Daddy." Firming her resolve, she rose to her feet and clasped Keaton's hand. His nod of support made her feel marginally better. "So we're doing this?"

"I don't believe we have a choice," Alastair replied as he worked the anklet through his fingers. "We're unable to contact the Goddess for permission, and the children need to be recalled."

"Not to mention, I want to go back to my time."

"That, too," he said to LJ.

The slider opened, and Aurora stepped into the room. She took one look at LJ and exclaimed, "Bloody hell!"

His expression was nothing short of poleaxed as he saw her lovely face. "Wh—?"

Amusement curled her uncle's mouth up at the corners, and his eyes gleamed with an oddly wicked satisfaction. "*This* is Aurora."

As if compelled, LJ crossed to her and stared down into her wide sky-blue eyes, his mouth still hanging slightly agape. With a shake of his head, he lifted his arm, prepared to touch her porcelain skin, only to have it captured by Uncle Alastair.

"I'll admit to feeling the same upon first seeing Rorie. However, I'll happily detach your wrist if you touch her."

"I would never!" But they all knew he'd been about to, regardless of his denial.

The stranger thing was her mother's inability to respond. It was as if she were equally enthralled.

"I believe you should grow a beard, brother," Preston said dryly. "Rorie seems to be fascinated by your rugged counterpart."

Straightening his tie, Alastair shot him a dirty look. "Bite your tongue, man!"

"Mama? Are you okay?" Spring asked.

Aurora shook her head slowly, as if waking from a

dream. "Yes. Yes, of course. I... The resemblance is extraordinary, isn't it?"

"Only if I failed to groom myself for weeks on end," Alastair answered with an arch look.

With a suddenness that surprised them all, Aurora laughed. Its light musical quality was a joy to listen to, and LJ once again looked like he'd been punched upside the head.

"I suppose you're sorry you never met my mother in your world," Autumn said with a small smile.

"But I have. She's my wife."

"Wait, what? I thought you said she married my father on the other side? That they..." She cast a look at her dad and grimaced, not wanting to reveal the death of his alternate-reality twin. "You said your wife's name is Angelica."

"Yes. Angelica Fennell," LJ replied. "Her parents visited the States when she was a teenager. I was smitten from the start."

"So who was Aurora Fennell to you?" Alastair asked in confusion.

"My sister-in-law. Angelica's youngest sibling who remained in England with her father's family."

"I only have a brother," Rorie said with a frown.

"You have no brother in my world."

Keaton shook his head, for the first time taking a good look at the newcomer in their midst. "I'm so goddamned confused."

"Right. You weren't here for that part. Lumberjack

Alastair came walking out of the woods when Uncle Al and I were calling Isis. He's who came to our side when our kids went through the portal," Autumn explained, rubbing the spot between her brows to dispel the forming headache. It was all too fucking much. She just wanted her kids home safe.

Doing a head count, she said, "We have enough to open the portal. Let's get the things we need."

8

Keaton went with Alastair and Lumberjack Al to Thorne Industries, and it occurred to him that this was his first visit to the business. It felt odd that he'd never been there, considering it was a constant topic of conversation in the months leading up to Aurora Fennell-Thorne's resurrection.

The place resembled any modernized industrial building, and from the outside, anyone passing by would think it was a standard company, with its mirrored floor-to-ceiling windows and enormous parking lot. Stepping inside, it seemed no different than any mortal corporation. However, Keaton knew what the unsuspecting didn't. Underneath this building was a giant vault containing magical artifacts held in trust for the Witches' Council.

Nash Thorne, Alastair's son, worked for the Council, and when he took over Thorne Industries upon Alastair's retirement, he'd turned the place into a stronghold. Something Alastair never would've done in *any* incarnation. This was made fact by the distasteful expression on LJ's countenance as he surveyed his surroundings inside the vault.

"My sentiments exactly," Alastair said aloud. "All these lovely items going to waste."

His roughneck twin chuckled, and the sound was opposite Alastair's unique bark-like laugh. Autumn had once told him her uncle had a hard life and little amusement as an adult. Clearly, the same couldn't be said for the alternate-reality version. Without the enemies and wars, his life had probably been fairly strife-free.

"Sperm Donor."

LJ's dark-blond brows shot up as they turned to find Nash Thorne lounging in the doorway of the secret vault. Although similar in appearance to his father, his expression was less arrogant. Blond with classical features, he bore the same old-Hollywood flare. Lent to his stunning looks was a fluidity of movement, as if he didn't hurry for anyone.

But there, the resemblance ended. Keaton knew Nash to be more studious, perhaps a bit absent-minded when he fell into his research. The man was also inherently kind, whereas Alastair didn't suffer fools. Keaton couldn't say he'd ever seen the elder Thorne be purposely cruel, unless it was to an enemy, but the guy would just as soon smite a person as let them roam free to strike again.

In that, they were similar. Keaton had learned to set aside any squeamishness when it came to those trying to hurt his family. His first instinct wasn't one of kill or be killed, but he'd definitely incapacitate someone until he discovered their motives. Autumn usually beat him to it, though.

"Son." Heavy humor hung in Alastair's tone. For most of their lives, he and Nash had been at odds. Mostly his son's doing. However, in recent years, they'd strengthened their familial bond, and their taunts were more lighthearted, meant to tease.

"What brings you by today? Not satisfied with the way I'm running the place?" Nash asked him, sending a curious look Keaton's way. He straightened when he glimpsed the third person in their party, and his face arrested in surprise. "Holy sh—uh, crap!"

"He cursed, too?" LJ murmured.

"Yep," Keaton said with a light laugh. "He has the ability to call trash pandas with a single swear word."

"Stuff it, Keat," Nash replied good-naturedly. "Someone want to tell me why there's a flannel-wearing clone of my father running about?"

"Perhaps we should adjourn to your office." Alastair didn't wait but led the way out of the vault, into the spacious executive suite. Without preamble, he said, "Your cousin's children opened a portal to an alternate reality, and we need the items I used to revive Rorie. Do you have them handy, son?"

"Yes, but they won't work for a portal without modification of the spell. But first, specifics. How in the world did two children open one without the tools? What spell did they use?"

"One from a copy of the *Book of Thoth*." Keaton sighed and shook his head. "I had no idea my parents had one in the ceremony room."

"An exact replica?" Nash frowned, appearing unconvinced such a thing existed.

"Spring seems to believe so," Alastair said, absently touching items on his son's desk and turning them so they were aligned a specific way.

Scowling, Nash crossed to the desk and rearranged what his father had moved.

A grin flashed across both Alastairs' faces before they sobered.

"I'm proof positive the young'uns were able to open it," LJ told Nash.

"Wait, so you're my father from the alternate reality?" A harsh bark of laughter escaped Nash as he stared hard at the other man. "Incredible. What happened to you?"

"The better question would be, what didn't?" Keaton said dryly. "But tell me why you don't think Jolly and Chloe could've opened the portal on their own."

"It would take more power than the two of them

have combined," Nash replied simply. "They don't have enough juice between them to pull it off."

"Even if Jolyon was untethered?" Alastair asked as he crossed his arms and leaned back against the desk. "Portals are rooted in Earth Witch magic, no?"

"Yes and no. They require both an Earth and an Air elemental. But I'm telling you, I honestly don't believe two small kids without knowledge could accomplish it, Dad. They don't have the skill needed to control the spell."

"But it is possible?" LJ said with a frown.

After a significant pause, Nash nodded. "I suppose anything is possible. Probable? No."

The answer was not what Keaton expected. "Then who could've opened it?"

Nash shot an expectant look at LJ. "Maybe you'd like to answer that?"

"I can't. I don't know." The sincerity in LJ's expression was confusing. As the one who'd traveled through the portal, he was the only person likely to have an agenda or the power. Yet looking at him now, he didn't seem to be the instigator of their problem.

"We'll have to get the details from Chloe when she returns. But can we please come up with a plan to get my children back?" Keaton wasn't beyond begging in his desperation.

Nash's expression was grim when he shook his head. "I don't know how to help you."

9

Keaton wanted to swear hard enough to conjure trash pandas, and it wasn't even his curse to bear. Running trembling fingers through his hair, he did his best not to scream his frustration.

"You and Spring are basically our only hope," he said to Nash.

"Not necessarily. You could call Damian Dethridge."

"The Aether?" The tone of Keaton's voice rose an octave. The idea of going to that powerful fucker was daunting. It wasn't as if he had cause to fear the man. Hell, the guy's child was Chloe's best friend. But the Aether was also judge and jury to those who abused magic—as Keaton's kids had just done—and he dreaded bringing this to Damian's attention.

"I can consult with him on your behalf," Alastair

said with a compassionate look. "His daughter has been naughty a time or two. He'll understand."

"Yeah, I get that, but I'm also worried he'll be forced to take action this time. You said yourself that the Goddess was blocked when you summoned her. That might be part of Jolly's doing." Dropping his chin to his chest, Keaton sighed and took a moment to compose himself. With three empaths present, he needed to get his fear under control. "What are we going to do?" he asked helplessly. "This is all my fault for leaving them unsupervised."

"We've all left our children unsupervised a time or two, my boy," Alastair replied gently. "You couldn't have anticipated they'd open a portal in the few minutes you were gone. Your daughter is old enough to know better." The last comment didn't come across as judgmental, merely as an observation, adding to Alastair's supportive statement. "I won't rest until your children are returned. I promise."

Deeply grateful but too emotional to verbally respond, Keaton nodded his thanks. He had little doubt Alastair would recognize his inability to speak and why.

The ring of his cellphone startled him out of his worrisome musings.

"Babe? Have you found something?" he asked his wife in lieu of a greeting as he switched the call to speaker.

"Spring may have," Autumn replied. "She said upon

further inspection of the book, she doesn't think it's an exact replica. More like some altered version that subverts deity intervention."

"*Fuck.*"

The chittering of raccoons filled the room.

"Sounds like my cousin isn't thrilled by the idea of this book," Autumn said with a hard laugh. "Tell him we aren't, either. I think you fellas need to return home."

"Be there momentarily." Keaton disconnected and tried not to laugh at the horror on LJ's face as the handful of trash pandas surrounded Nash. Their bandit-like faces all stared up at him as if he were a god and they awaited his command with bated breath.

With a resigned sigh, Nash conjured a bowl of peanuts and allowed them to scoop out whatever they could carry before he waved a hand and returned them to where they'd come.

"That right there is disturbin' as hell," LJ declared with a shake of his head. "Those things could be rabid."

"Not really. If I detect illness, I heal them. It's the least I can do if they're showing up to offer assistance." Color crept up Nash's neck as his father laughed outright. "Don't act like you wouldn't do the same, Sperm Donor."

Alastair didn't reply, but he smirked, which was mostly the same thing.

"We have to go, guys," Keaton reminded them.

"Your home?" Nash asked. When Keaton nodded,

he said, "Go on, and I'll follow after I let my wife know I'll be gone for the rest of the day. Tell Spring to text me with any artifacts she may need between now and when I get there."

"Will do."

They left from inside Nash's office, not bothering to go out the way they came. Keaton was too keyed up to put on an act, and if he didn't take action soon, he'd lose his goddamned mind.

AUTUMN PACED the living room as Keaton and the two Alastairs brought everyone up to speed on their conversation with Nash. With every second her children were gone, she unraveled a little bit more. Soon, she'd be a complete basket case and rip the veil apart with her bare hands. Or she would if it were possible.

"Can we hurry this up, gang?" she snapped. "I'm freaking the fuck out here."

Spring looked at her as if she wanted to give her a hug, but feared having her arm torn off. In their father's eyes was a deep understanding, and Autumn couldn't meet his gaze, or she'd cry. He'd been through it when Spring was abducted and held for months on end, with none of them able to find or rescue her. When she'd returned to their home, she was changed, remembering none of them. The Thornes' enemy chose well when he'd selected

Spring to bring them to their knees. To this day, none of her family wished to discuss that excruciating time.

Alastair rose to his feet. "I'm going to step out and call Damian. Nash should be here soon—ah, there he is. Show him what you found, child, and I'll let you know what Dethridge has to say." In minutes, he was back, and his expression was blank, as if he was trying to hide his deeper emotions.

Autumn wanted to throw up.

"Give it to us straight, Mr. Thorne," Keaton said with heavy resignation in his voice.

"It's not good. He's never known this to happen, and already, there is buzz through the Witches' Council and the Authority," Alastair replied, darting a significant glance at Preston. "We need to correct this within the hour, or those in charge will have no choice but to step in. They recommended we don't use the same spell."

"Then what the hell are we to use?" Keaton demanded, forgetting himself in the face of his worry. Surprisingly, Alastair didn't chastise him for his disrespect.

"I didn't say we wouldn't use it, simply that they recommended we don't." A wicked gleam of intent entered her uncle's eyes, and he slowly surveyed the crowd. "Anyone opposed?"

Not one of them objected.

Thornes hated to be told what to do as a rule, and

if it involved one of their own, they held tight to the saying, "Damn the torpedoes! Full speed ahead!"

"Let's go get Jolyon and Chloe," he said with an encouraging grin for Autumn.

Until the instant he said it, she hadn't been aware of holding her tension in her shoulders, and they dropped along with her anxiety.

Finally!

The necessary action would be taken to retrieve her children.

10

Autumn led the way downstairs. She was closely followed by Keaton, the two Alastairs, her father, Spring, and Knox.

Spring notified them that Summer was on her way to examine Lazy Jay and add her healing touch to Keaton's. Autumn's in-laws had volunteered to stay with the horses to make sure there were no further developments or illness popping up.

Founder was rare in their barn, but it could happen, like in the case of Lazy Jay. He was one of three thoroughbreds Keaton had recently rescued from neglect, and Lazy Jay was doing everything in his power to make up for not having enough food in the past. Now, he preferred to overeat and under exercise, putting a strain on his feet.

As cold as it seemed, Autumn couldn't spare any more worry for the horse because her primary concern required all her attention. Once they were all gathered around the altar, Spring opened the book to the page they believed the children had used.

"There's no magical signature," LJ said almost absently as he studied the book over Autumn's shoulder.

As one, her family turned to stare at him.

He lifted his brows in response. "Trace elements of your kids' raw magic are in the room, but I don't see any attached to *that* particular page."

Autumn shared a look with Alastair before she addressed LJ's comment. "Are you saying you can *see* magic?"

With a confused frown, his gaze systematically touched on each of them as if he were studying the group for truthfulness. Finally, he turned to Alastair.

"Witches have a natural empathic ability to see auras. Why can't y'all see the magic in the air?"

"Another magical being's power is discernible in their aura, yes. We can all *feel* the magic in the air. Other than the occasional object, however, I don't believe I've ever witnessed the glow of previously used magic. Was it something you were taught?" Alastair asked curiously.

"No. It comes natural to us."

"Us being Thornes?" Autumn asked LJ.

"Yes. Anyone as gifted as we are should have that ability."

"Interesting." Her father stepped forward and

slowly thumbed through the book. "What about any other page or spell?"

About five turns later, LJ touched Preston's wrist. "There."

When Autumn read what was on the page, she nearly fainted. "They were trying to call up a Cerberus? What the actual fuck?" With a glare for LJ, she asked, "Are you kidding me right now? Is this a joke to you?"

"Afraid not. They actually exist in our world." When she gave a disbelieving scoff, he said, "How do you think you know about them, Tums? Because somewhere, sometime in history, one crossed through the portal. You've no idea how difficult that bastard was to get back."

"But legend reported it was to guard Hades," Spring said. "No one believes they're *real*."

"Yet they are, and your clone has one," he replied grimly. "Your niece and nephew are likely with your counterpart if they tried that spell, and I can promise you, girl, that woman isn't as nice as you appear to be."

"Why? What went wrong in her life that she turned evil?"

He shot Preston a sour look for asking the question. "She had absentee parents and fell in with the wrong crowd."

"There's a bad witch crowd?" Autumn shared an amused glance with her sister. "You'd think my twin would've been the one to turn to the dark side."

"There's still time," Alastair said dryly. "Now, enough of this. Cast the same spell, and let's get going."

"We need to find the other person or thing that crossed through the portal first," LJ told him.

"Wait, what?" Autumn pressed her fingers to her closed lids as her head began to pound. The last thing she needed was a damned migraine to top off the day.

Nash had joined them during LJ's last comment. "For every one thing that passes through, another is transported here," he told her, then gestured to her uncle and Keaton. "Didn't they tell you that?"

"We didn't detail that part of the conversation," her husband confessed.

Using her thumb to indicate LJ, she said, "I thought *he* was the trade."

"Sorry, hon. But I'm gonna suggest you've got a three-headed dog wandering your woods," LJ replied. "And the bitch of it is that they have a natural-born cloaking ability. You won't see one unless it wants you to."

"Tell me this is a nightmare I'm going to wake from soon." She sighed as she stretched the tension from her neck. "Keaton, call Coop and tell him to be on the lookout for this thing, or rather evidence of this thing." With a questioning look for Knox, she asked, "You saw no giant poop piles anywhere around when you went to look for them initially?"

Despite the severity of the situation, Knox laughed. "None, but Keat called me back right away."

With a nod, she took a screenshot of the spell. "I'm going to call it to me with a slight modification."

"I can help with that one," Spring offered. "I—"

Their attention was caught by a shuffling and a growl from the top of the stairs. When Autumn ducked her head around the corner to peer upward, she sucked in her breath. "Found it," she croaked. "Don't know how it got in the house, but it's here now."

"Likely it was nappin' somewhere close by," LJ told her, turning thoughtful eyes on the beast.

"That explains the oddball indentation on the daybed," Autumn murmured.

The thing was gigantic. Solid black, it was the size of a Mastiff on steroids. Each of its three pairs of eyes were focused directly on her. Jaws agape, the beast drooled yellow-tinted saliva onto the floor, and it made a hissing sound with every droplet that hit the ground.

"Is its saliva toxic?" There wasn't much she feared, but acid spit ranked at the top if she were being forced to make a list.

"Yes," LJ replied grimly. "Don't let it bite or lick you."

"Lick? Is it just being friendly or testing for taste?"

"They've been known to do both."

Alastair moved to stand beside LJ, jockeying positions with Autumn. "Let's find out, shall we?"

Surprising them all, he whistled and smiled at the

beast. "Come, Cerberus. Come, uh,"—he shifted his head and looked toward the underside of the dog—"girl."

The monstrous canine studied him for a moment, judging his worth, then she tucked her heads and whined.

"I think the openin' is too small for her to get downstairs." LJ spread his arms wide, and the walls shifted as the steps lengthened, creating a larger staircase. "Call her again."

"Impressive," Alastair murmured with a nod of his head. "I'll need to try that when I have more time."

"It's simple enough."

The beast inched down the steps, her eyes locked on the two Alastairs. When she'd reached the bottom, she gave everyone a wary look.

"Are they mistreated in your world?" Alastair asked his twin in a low voice. "She appears to be skittish."

"Their acidic saliva makes them unwelcome in most cases."

"I see." To the beast, he said, "Let's do something about that, shall we?"

"You plannin' to turn wine to water, so to speak?"

With a cheerful grin, Alastair approached the beast. "Exactly that, LJ."

11

Keaton had never witnessed anything like the two formidable warlocks, essentially clones from different worlds, casually talking about a three-headed monster as if they were discussing tie colors.

Inching forward, he gripped Autumn's hand and drew her farther back, behind the others. Her fingers tightened over his in understanding, but her gaze remained locked on the giant canine.

With no concern for his own welfare, Alastair tugged up his pants legs and squatted, then held out a hand. The beast's wicked jaws clamped shut, and she tentatively stretched forward to sniff. Lowering her head, she lifted solemn eyes to his as if she feared to trust.

"I won't hurt you, lovely lady," Alastair said in a soothing, seductive voice.

As if she understood, the mutant canine inched closer.

"Knox, please be ready to stop the saliva as it drops. This is my favorite suit, and I wouldn't care to have it ruined."

Keaton's mouth dropped open even as his wife snorted her amusement.

"He's crazy," he muttered beneath his breath.

"Not at all, my boy," Alastair answered in Autumn's stead. "I merely don't take life as seriously as you do. No one gets out of it alive."

LJ grinned. "I like you more and more, tight-ass."

"I'll go to my grave with a smile on my face, knowing I have your admiration," Alastair deadpanned.

"Darling, I don't mean to hurry you along, but my grandchildren are wandering without supervision." Aurora placed a hand on her husband's shoulder. "You know what Thornes are like when left unattended."

"Indeed I do, my love. The evidence is staring us right in the face."

"Yes, well, work your—well, for lack of a better word—*magic* on the thing and be done with it."

The dog-like creature inched forward until her massive center head was only a foot from Alastair. The other two heads were pointed outward, as if to keep guard should anyone else move toward her.

The one facing LJ whimpered as it gazed up at him, and frowning, he squatted beside Alastair, fearlessly extending his hand to stroke between her eyes. Those same eyes closed in bliss as her jowly mouth turned upward and her tongue lolled out, spilling more sizzling saliva onto the floor.

"I think someone's in love," Autumn quipped. "Why am I not surprised you could charm the wild out of a Cerberus?"

"It's one of my many talents," Alastair and LJ replied at the same time. They paused to exchange a highly amused glance, then concentrated on the monstrous acid-dripping dog.

"You must be confused, girl," LJ said softly. "Everything's different than you're used to, huh? I feel the same. How 'bout we take care of your little droolin' issues and get you back home?"

The three-headed canine promptly sat on her haunches.

"We're going to do a nifty little spell, and then you'll get all the lovin' your big ol' heart desires."

Her tail, the size of a battleship's towline, swished back and forth in her agreement.

Spring moved through their awestruck crowd and handed Alastair a piece of paper. "This spell should do what you need it to," she told him.

He took a moment to study it, then nodded. "Thank you, child. I agree. This should work nicely."

"You don't need to cast a circle, Uncle, unless your new friend is protected by magic."

"I hadn't thought about that." Alastair gave the

beast a considering look. "I believe you understand me well enough, lovely lady," he told the dog. "I'm going to send a light current your way. Don't be frightened."

It was the damnedest thing, but the Cerberus cocked her heads, and hers was an expression of understanding. She stood perfectly still as Alastair stretched his fingertips to shoot a test wave her way. A blue crackling light appeared between them and was gone an instant later.

"She's got magic of her own, but she's not protected. We'll be able to neutralize her saliva."

Keaton sighed his relief. "Great. Let's get on with this, please. My anxiety is at an all-time high."

Within minutes, the Cerberus's drool was as harmless as any old pup, and she tried her best to become a three-hundred-pound lapdog, with all her affection directed toward the two Alastairs.

"This feels like a bizarre dream," Keaton murmured to his wife. "What is happening right now?"

"I don't know, but I'm heading to the clearing. The pull is strong."

Autumn faced Alastair. "Bring your new bestie, and let's go."

Other than a lifted brow for her commanding tone, he didn't react.

"Sorry," she muttered. "This is taking too long."

"Agreed. Lead the way."

The kindness in his eyes eased her fear that she'd offended him, and she spared a second to hug him, offering her thanks. His answer was a kiss on her temple.

When their small group arrived at the clearing, two things struck Autumn at once. The first was that there was no movement. No wind, no forest sounds, and no smell associated with the trees. The second was the presence of a stronger magical creature than any of their group.

"Something's here," Preston said, lifting his arms and conjuring fireballs. With the flames dancing in both palms, he turned in a slow circle as he studied the tree line. "There's an 'off' feel to the place. Anyone else sense it?"

"Yes. I believe we all do, brother," Alastair replied. Removing his suit jacket, he placed it on the altar, then followed with the removal of his tie.

"You know it's serious when Alastair Thorne removes his tie," Knox said lightly. But he, too, was on high alert, and although he held his arms low, he quickly drew molecules from the air to compress them into the electrical weapon he was creating to protect their group.

"Stand ready, fellas," LJ said. "This is what I felt before getting shoved through the portal."

"Are you saying one is about to—"

The entire clearing turned dark, and it was as if someone had shut off the lights in a small closet with no windows. Pitch black, and Autumn could see nothing. Hear no one. She reached for Keaton's hand and came up empty.

"Babe?"

Her call was lost in the void, as if the sound never left her throat.

Panic clawed at her insides, and her heart throbbed loudly in her ears, making her deaf to anything but the pounding.

"Keaton?" she shouted. "Dad? Anyone?"

Again, nothing.

around them. Each of them was divided by a type of invisible bubble, with the exception of LJ and the Cerberus. They were the only two with the freedom to move among their group.

"Can you hear me, LJ?" she shouted.

He mouthed the word "yes" and nodded simultaneously. Gesturing with his hand for her to turn down the volume, he mouthed, "Too loud."

"I can't hear you," she said in a normal voice. "Can you conjure pen and paper and tell me what the hell is happening?"

Doing as she asked, he wrote his reply. *"Don't know."*

"Fucking lovely," she grumbled.

Her attention was caught by a movement behind him, and she called her warning. He spun to see what was coming just as the Cerberus lowered her heads. The fur along her spine lifted, and her thick tail stilled until she seemingly recognized the newcomers.

A Gothic version of Spring stepped into the clearing, followed by another Cerberus that was, if possible, twice the size of LJ's new pet. The creature dwarfed Goth Spring, making her look no bigger than a child's doll guarded by a faithful hound.

Sauntering forward, she eyed their group curiously. When she saw this world's Spring, she misstepped, and her clunky black platform shoes came to an abrupt halt. Her shock appeared short-lived, and she approached Spring's bubble. With a simple touch of her finger, it popped, reminding Autumn of the soap bubbles from Jolly's evening baths.

"You're a Goody Two-shoes," Gothica stated flatly.

Unsurprisingly, Autumn's sister laughed. "Am I?"

Their voices echoed inside Autumn's cocoon and sounded like they were coming through a 1960s radio with shitty reception. Why she could hear *them* and not LJ was a curious matter to ponder at a later date.

"If you want to call me that, I'm cool with it," Spring told Gothica. "But I've been known to bury a bastard or two when crossed."

Grudging respect lit Gothica's dark jade eyes before her attention was caught by Knox. Inside his bubble, he was frantic. He threw lightning bolt after lightning bolt at the barrier wall in his helpless need to get to his mate.

"Wow!" Fearlessly, she approached his invisible cage. "Aren't you a gorgeous piece of man flesh?"

"Man flesh?" Spring grinned at her counterpart when the woman cast a glance over her shoulder. "I'm not objecting to the name. It's absolutely fitting. I might adopt it for myself." To Knox, she said, "What do you think, babe?"

His narrow-eyed response caused both Springs to laugh.

"He's yours?"

"He is," Spring replied with a loving smile for Knox.

Gothica actually appeared disappointed.

"You and the Knox of your world don't hook up, I'm assuming." Autumn's sister offered up a sympathetic look. "That's sad."

"Never met anyone named Knox." With a shrug, Gothica faced her uncle. "Alastair. Why aren't I surprised you've upset the balance between worlds?"

"Not me." He hooked a thumb in Autumn's direction. "Your sister's kids."

Gothic Spring approached her bubble and popped it to allow Autumn her freedom. "Your *kids*? Plural? I'm surprised you and Keaton had more than your first witchy wonder. That spoiled brat is the bane of my existence."

"Watch it, Gothica," Autumn warned in an icy tone. "I don't know what the fuck you're talking about, but I can promise you, no child of mine is a spoiled brat."

A calculating gleam lit the other woman's eyes. "Her name is Rachel, and I promise you, she is. She's your mini-me and thinks her shit don't stink."

Never mind that her brain was reeling from the fact she had a daughter named Rachel, Autumn couldn't wrap her head around the fact her younger sister's clone was a raging bitch. "So she's tough. What's wrong with that? It wasn't a crime the last time I checked."

"It's a crime when she terrorizes a town of innocents. But you and your lazy-ass boyfriend can't be bothered to rein her in."

The last bit caught her off guard. "Boyfriend?"

"Mike, Max, Mark… whatever the hell his name is." Gothic Spring shrugged, and Autumn cast a dark glance LJ's way.

"I thought you said I was married to Keaton?"

"You are," he replied matter-of-factly. "I didn't say you didn't run around on him."

The knowledge was a gut punch. Was everyone miserable in this alternate reality? How truly sad if that were the case. Dismissing the tragedy of their world, Autumn faced Gothic Spring.

"*My* children seem to have opened a portal to your world. I need to find them and bring them home."

Gothica's overpainted brows clashed. "Shit."

"Shit? What shit? The sound of your 'shit' is ominous."

"I thought she was lying again."

"She?"

"Rachel."

"I don't know Rachel. I only know that my daughter, Chloe, and my son, Jolyon, are lost in your time."

"She did say her name was Chloe," Gothic Spring said with a scrunched nose followed by an uncaring shrug. "I guess I should've questioned her before—"

"Before what?" Tone lethal, Autumn was ready to tear the bitch a new asshole.

The look Gothica turned on her was regretful with a sprinkle of wariness mixed in.

Forgetting for a moment that an acid-drooling dog the size of a small house had the woman's back, Autumn grabbed her by the collar of her drab black dress and hauled her close. Nose to nose, she snarled, "What the fuck did you do to my kids?"

13

This chapter has gone the way of all the Thorne Witches' Chapter 13s. Take a break, stretch, then dig back in for the second half of this adventuresome story.

14

Keaton couldn't comprehend everything happening. There were two Alastairs, two Springs, two daughters, and two behemoth Cerberuses. Two worlds had collided, and everything around him was unreal and unimaginable.

Autumn had taken a lover?

Okay, yeah, not *his* Autumn, but still. She wasn't the type to sneak around.

He stared at her. Hard.

Or maybe she was.

If she'd done it in that world, couldn't she do it in his? Would she suddenly recall she'd once believed he deserved payback for what occurred during their breakup? It made his old firebombed truck seem like child's play. She definitely could've done worse. Watching her now, as she shook her sister's twin like a rag doll and demanded answers, he knew he'd gotten off lightly.

Christ, she was beautiful. An auburn-haired Amazon warrior who put Wonder Woman to shame.

Dismissing the unease caused by learning there was a cheating replica of his wife, Keaton focused on the situation at hand—the bubble encapsulating him.

He touched it from the inside and experienced a small jolt. Nothing shocking, more of a simple power surge. The surface was odd, as if it had a gritty, sand-like texture, and yet it was clear.

But the ocean could wash away sand.

As a water elemental, Keaton wasn't able to draw forth the actual sea this far inland, but he could probably pull water up from the earth to erode enough of the wall and make good his escape. There was no time left to wonder if the darker version of Spring intended to release them to get to Chloe and Jolly, and it boiled down to his children's safety first.

Squatting, Keaton placed his palms flat on the ground, and concentrating all his attention on the act itself, he called the moisture from the ground to him. It wouldn't do to remove all the liquid from the soil at once, or he could potentially create a sinkhole for himself. As soon as he was sure he had enough to work with, he redirected the water toward the bottom of the textured barrier, creating a small pool and lapping it against the wall like waves on the beach.

He glanced up in time to see his wife's fist connect with the woman from the alternate dimension, knocking her down and out. The Cerberus growled and loomed over Autumn as the sound fizzled out in Keaton's bubble.

In an instant, his wife conjured a wooden canopy to protect herself from the monster's saliva.

From his vantage point, he could tell it wouldn't last long. Her mouth moved, but he couldn't make out what she was saying. Frustration gripped him, and he redoubled his efforts with the water against the wall, raising it higher for a bigger opening. Was it working? It was too difficult to tell, but it did seem as if the colors on the other side of the wall weren't as muted as the parts he'd left alone.

Wildly, he looked around to see what the others might be doing to escape. Alastair was using Keaton's same process, and Spring was examining Preston's enclosure as if to understand the magic her clone had used to create it in the first place.

A grin curled her mouth, and the next second, she pressed her palms to the exterior wall, causing it to disintegrate and sand to rain down on her father's head.

With a sweep of her hand, she took down all the bubbles at once.

Keaton dove for Autumn right as her wooden shield developed its first hole. Dragging her to safety, he shouted over his shoulder to Alastair.

"Do what you did to the other one! Like yesterday, man!"

He hadn't realized Autumn's spell was also keeping the ferocious canine at bay until he could feel the thing breathing down his neck.

Autumn screamed her pain, and he turned in time to see her arch her back.

A shout echoed through the clearing, and the Cerberus thudded to a halt, swinging its heads in the direction of the others.

Acting on instinct, Keaton tugged Autumn into his arms and hollered, "Hold your breath!"

He conjured a continuous deluge of water, hoping to neutralize the acid. In his inexperience and panic, it felt like the force of ten waterfalls, and it knocked them to the ground. He did his best to protect Autumn's head as it hammered down upon them.

"Pull it back, babe!" she shouted, coughing between words as water filled her mouth. "Pull it back!"

Closing his eyes, he pictured a gentle shower.

Her beaming smile was his reward. "Well done, Keat."

"How's your back?" She shifted for him to look, and Keaton winced at the angry splotches marring her previously silky skin. "Jesus!"

"It probably looks worse than it is," she said with a wry smile. The pain in her eyes belied her words.

"We'll see what Spring has for healing. If she doesn't, I'm sure Winnie will prepare something for when we return. Can I take your pain away? Tell me what to do."

"I don't want to bother Win. She's got enough on her plate with the boys." Autumn rose to her feet, and her expression arrested to one of wariness.

Keaton turned his head to see the approaching alternate-reality Spring. The woman's visage was technically the same as his sister-in-law, but where their Spring was pure of heart and intent, the other's trials had hardened her eyes and turned down her mouth at the edges.

When she reached Autumn, there was the smallest bit of contrition in the way her lips twisted up and her gaze softened. "It seems I owe you an apology, sister from another mister."

His wife's brows shot up, but she remained watchful.

"I didn't mean to make it seem like anything had happened to Ra—uh, Chloe or your son. The girl showed up at my home, and I sent her away, assuming it was a game Rachel was playing." The woman frowned as she met Autumn's stare. "I'm not lying. I never do."

"I didn't say you were, but why the hell would you send a young girl and her brother away? There had to be a small part of you that recognized she was frantic."

"Your son wasn't with her, and Rachel has thought to play me before, Autumn. But it's neither here nor there. I can take you to her now, and then we can find your boy."

Keaton reached for her arm when she shifted away. The reverberating growl of the woman's guardian sent a chill along his nerve endings. Slowly, he lifted his hands in the air, showing the beast he meant no harm.

"Sorry, lady. I acted before I thought," he said with a cautious glance at the monster dog.

"Same old Keaton," she said. Her eyes had cooled, and the disgusted look on her beautiful face told him she hated his counterpart from her world.

"Actually, I'm not. I care very much about my wife and children. I was just going to ask you how we could get through the portal as easily as you did."

Her laugh was brittle. "You already did, bud. Your entire group crossed the boundary, straight into my clearing. Why do you think you stumbled into my traps?"

"Wait! What?" Autumn's skin turned ghostly pale. "We're on *your* plane? All of us?"

When the alternate-reality Spring nodded, Keaton and Autumn shared a horrified look.

"Who went through to our side?" they asked in unison.

"If I had to guess, more of Philomena's puppies," Gothica replied.

The three-headed beast let out a mournful cry.

"Puppies?"

"Like the one you entered with. That's one of hers."

"That thing's a *puppy*?" Keaton gaped at the animal in question, then did a headcount of their group. "So if nine souls crossed here, nine acid-dripping puppies went there?"

"Well, at least five of them. That's all the puppies she had. Cerberuses have litters in multiples of three. You had one, and the other five are missing. It's why I came to the clearing to look for them."

"But that's not enough!" Keaton's insides churned. They didn't have a way to notify Coop of the potential problem. "What the hell else did we send through?"

15

"I'm sorry for punching you in the face," Autumn said a few minutes later as Gothica spread a salve on her back. The woman refused to use actual magic to heal her, stating she'd shunned using it unless she had no choice.

"I probably deserved it," Gothica replied shortly.

"You didn't. I've got a hair-trigger temper, and I'm itching to find my kids."

Silence greeted her comment, but the fingers on her back gentled.

"Why are you estranged from the family, Gothica?"

The other woman choked off a laugh. "Gothica?"

"Sorry. You've got the whole goth thing going, with the black clothes and chunky-heeled shit stompers. The name helps me keep you and my sister, uh, the other Spring, separate in my mind."

"Gothica." A snort sounded behind her. "Fitting."

"So? The family thing?"

The woman took a long moment to screw the lid on her salve tin, then another to put it in the messenger bag slung over her shoulder. Just when Autumn thought she wouldn't answer, Gothica said, "I think my life was probably a little harder than your sister's."

Autumn scoffed. "I doubt that."

"Did your parents cast her out for dabbling in the dark arts?" As if she understood she was being waspish, Gothica cleared her throat. "When you have an insatiable mind, you want to know everything. I fell in with a group of rebellious witches who believed the Authority was made up of a bunch of asshats determined to mind control us."

"*You* believe in mind control?" Autumn asked disbelievingly. Her gaze met solemn jade eyes.

"No. But it was nice to have the freedom to do what I wanted instead of what was expected. Of what came with the Thorne name." Gothica focused on the leather tie attached to the bag, working it until Autumn was convinced it would tear off. "There were other beings with capabilities far beyond those of an average witch, and I needed to know how that worked. Why they were given certain gifts over others."

Gothica's passion for knowledge was reflected in her voice. The longing to learn, evident in the searching glance she cast Spring's way.

"You're misunderstood." Autumn didn't mean to blurt it, but it surprised her to see the lost, lonely person her own sister might've been had she not received guidance. "But where were the rest of us? Where was I? Summer? Winnie?"

"I don't know anyone named Summer. Winnie?" A quicksilver flash of pain crossed her face. "If you mean our sister, Winter, she left a long time ago. When I was still a kid. No one's heard from her in years."

"Summer doesn't exist?" An ache started in Autumn's chest. What would her life have been without their fourth sister? The sunshine and laughter Summer added to their lives were immeasurable. "There were only the three of us?"

Gothica nodded. "This world's Autumn hooked up with Keaton right out of college, and Winnie took off in high school. And our parents left for an extended tour of Europe, where they died. It's just me. Whenever I tried to tag along with Autumn and Keaton, she sent me home."

"Jesus, hon. I'm so sorry." LJ caught her attention in the distance as he gestured toward the direction of Thorne Manor. "What about him? He seems pretty cool."

"He tried to take me in, but his wife's a bit of a bitch."

"His wife is our mother in my world," Autumn replied with a hard laugh. "The one with the short black hair, just there, talking to Uncle Alastair and LJ."

"Who's LJ?"

"Lumberjack Alastair. It's the flannel shirt and beard. He's made it way too easy for me to nickname him."

Gothica laughed, and the sound was as sweet as Spring's, but it was short-lived, as if the woman surprised herself with her display of amusement. But a wicked grin lingered, and she said, "That name is totally going to stick after you're gone."

Autumn fist bumped her. "That's what I'm talking about. Now, how about we find my kids, then you and I can have a sit-down and chat about what we can do to make your life better?"

"What's wrong with my life?"

As far as accidentally stepping in shit went, Autumn had jumped in with both feet. "I didn't mean it quite like it sounded. Only that I want to be sure you have everything you need. Maybe help you get rid of any darkness from the black arts so you can feel free to use your abilities as intended."

With a grudging nod, Gothica led the way back to the others in Autumn's group.

"When I saw Ra—uh, Chloe, she was wearing a blue top and jeans. There was a hole in one knee and twigs in her hair, but other than that, she seemed to be okay."

"Which direction did she run off to?"

"The Carlyle cabin."

"Cabin? Not estate?" Keaton asked sharply.

"Estate?" Gothica laughed again, and it was pure hilarity. "Those good-for-nothing Carlyles couldn't be bothered with the upkeep of an estate." Her perfect nose scrunched as she eyed Keaton, who had been silent until now. "Sorry, bud, but it's true."

Keaton opened his mouth to reply, but whatever he'd intended to say was cut short when the ground beneath them rumbled.

A child's angry scream sounded in the distance, and the trembling earth shook harder.

"Jolyon!" Alastair shouted over the roar of the earthquake. "We have to get his anklet back on him."

Staggering and scrambling to maintain her footing, Autumn bolted for the trees, screaming her son's name.

16

"Can you mitigate the quake?" Alastair shouted his question to the two Springs. "Work together to stop or lessen the effect of Jolyon's temper tantrum?"

Keaton stared. Or he would've had he not been watching for falling trees. "How do you know it's a temper—" Holding up a hand, he shook his head. "Forget it," he hollered over the noise. "Empath. I get it. You can feel him all this way, or was it the scream?"

"Both."

The ground stopped rumbling, and the sudden stillness was eerie as hell. As was the silence. Keaton ran toward the direction Autumn had taken, hoping to find his wife and children. Before entering the woods, he caught a flash of blue from the corner of his eye. The same color shirt as his daughter had been wearing just that morning.

Veering right, he jogged through the woods. "Chloe?"

When his daughter lifted her dirty, tear-stained face, Keaton's heart spasmed and went into overdrive. He rushed forward, only to stop when trepidation filled her eyes and her mouth contorted to scream.

"Chloe?"

"You're not my dad," she cried, scrambling backward and colliding with the tree trunk she'd been curled against.

"Yes, I am." Keaton held up his hands and slowly approached. "Why wouldn't you think so?"

"You're trying to trick me again."

Again? What the actual fuck?

"Who tricked you, sweetheart? Someone who looked like me?"

A frown marred her young visage, and she slowly edged her head sideways to survey the area around them. When she glanced back at him, she paid special attention to his clothes and hair.

Still, she remained silent on the subject of trickery, as if she didn't trust him.

"Midge, it's me. I promise."

"Daddy?" Her deep honey-colored eyes flew wide as she jumped up and rushed into his arms.

Sobs wracked her slender frame as she apologized over and over in a discombobulated babble. As much as he needed to find Autumn and Jolly, he also needed to let Chloe give into her deeper feelings and not try to shut her down. She'd survived a terrifying experience, and as the adult who'd aged ten years in the hours she was gone, he had to rein in his own emotions to allow for hers.

As he held her, he sent a big fucking "thank you" to the deities who'd been watching over her. Other than her apparent upset, she appeared to have weathered her mishap physically.

Chloe's tears slowed, and she got control of her hiccuping sobs. When only sniffles were left, he drew away to study her distraught countenance.

"All good, sweetheart?"

She nodded, but the tragic eyes she turned on him told a different story.

"Want to talk about it as we go find your mom and Jolly?"

"Mom's here?"

"She is." He grinned and tweaked a lock of her lank hair. "You didn't think she'd leave you to your own devices, do you?"

"I thought she'd be mad about, er, Jolly."

"What do you mean?"

Her gaze dropped to the dirt, and she gave a one-shouldered shrug so similar to Autumn's, he had to chuckle. She'd definitely picked up on his wife's mannerisms since Autumn came to live with them. But he wasn't surprised. She'd been Chloe's hero from the moment she sacrificed herself in the Otherworld so Chloe and Derrick could return home unscathed.

"Chloe?"

"I didn't think it would be bad to let him conjure a dog. He was scared, and I thought it might protect us when you and Mom weren't around."

Keaton had to check his immediate irritation at her accusatory tone. It felt unfounded. Wasn't she the one who always begged for more responsibility, insisting she was capable of caring for Jolly? "But I was only in the barn, midge."

"People can break in. Bad people who hate witches," she argued.

Understanding dawned.

A few years back, she'd believed she was safe in the park until she was approached by one of the Thornes' greatest enemies. The man had tried to abduct her that day, and if it weren't for Chloe's friend Derrick and fast action on the Thornes' part, the guy would've succeeded. Although nothing like that had happened in the intervening years, she still worried it might.

"So, how about, when we get home, we adopt a dog?" he suggested with an indulgent smile.

Her eyes flew wide in her incredulity. "You mean it?"

"As long as it's okay with your mom, I don't see why not."

"Oh, Daddy!" She flung herself at him, wrapping her skinny arms around his neck, and although she was choking the shit out of him with her gratitude, he didn't mind. "Thank you! Thank you!"

Just as dark spots danced behind his lids, he knew it was time to end their embrace. He'd be no use to anyone if he passed out from lack of air. Detangling himself, he swept her up and tossed her onto his back.

"Hang on, midge. We need to find the others."

He turned in time to see Gothica watching them with a bemused expression.

"You're not going to put us in a bubble again, are you?" he asked.

Her brows slammed together until she realized he was teasing. Wonder lit her face, and her gaze darted between him and Chloe.

"You're so different from the one here," she said softly, almost sweetly.

"Yeah, well, I'd like to have words with that dickhead before I leave." Keaton turned his head slightly to address his daughter. "Never repeat what I said. You shouldn't call people names."

"Even if they *are* a dickhead?" Gothica quipped, showing Keaton she had a sense of humor to match Spring's.

"She's allowed to think it, but not say it. Not until she's an adult, anyway."

Chloe giggled in his ear, but sobered as Gothica approached.

"I'd like to apologize, Chloe," the woman said. "I believed you were my niece playing an inappropriate prank. If I'd have known you entered the portal and were lost, I would never have turned you away."

12

The suspended sensation was similar to death, and Autumn worried for a moment that she'd been involved in a battle she couldn't remember. Were the deities deciding her fate as she waited in the Otherworld's holding room?

Goddess, she hoped not. She needed to see her children safe first.

A low humming started and grew louder with every beat of her heart until the noise was a pounding tempo in her brain. Where had she heard it before? Why did it seem familiar?

A golden glow filled the area around her, and she shielded her eyes from the glaring light. When it calmed to a candlelight-like illumination, she lowered her arm and lifted her lids. All around her, her family stood, poised as she was and taking in the scene

"Really?" Chloe asked, wariness in her voice.

"Really." Holding out a hand, Gothica smiled. "Will you forgive me?"

Reaching across Keaton's shoulder, his daughter accepted the offered hand and apology. "Thank you, Miss Spring."

Gothica's smile widened. "Let's go find your family."

As they trudged through the woods, Keaton thought about how bizarrely different their two worlds were. Pondered how their alternate-reality counterparts could be so drastic in personality from those on their side, to the point of leaving children to survive on their own without help. It was sad.

Chloe's arms tightened, warning him of trouble, and he shifted to shoot her a questioning look. Turning his head to the left, he noticed his doppelganger leaning drunkenly against a tree. As Keaton paused, so did the other man, and the beer bottle in his hand was suspended mid drink. His face was bloated from excess, and his blue eyes were flat.

"What did he say to you, midge?"

"He told me to stop crying like a baby and get lost. He called me Rachel. Like Miss Spring."

Setting her on the ground, he curled a hand around her nape and drew her close. After pressing a kiss to the top of her head, he said, "Stay here, sweetheart. I'm going to have a word with myself."

Gothica's grin transformed her pretty face to stunningly beautiful, and Keaton realized what had been missing: her twin's sweet, fun-loving personality. With a wink in her direction, he headed off toward the asshole version of himself.

"Hey, dickhead," he said in a patently false friendly tone.

The Neanderthal Keaton scowled and straightened from holding the tree up. "Who the fuck are you?"

"Father of the little girl you were a fucking asshole to, and I'd like to talk to you about that."

Without another word, Keaton clocked him.

17

Finding Jolyon wasn't difficult. Autumn simply followed his bellows until she caught sight of his light. A woman, the replica of her mother, was squatting next to him, dangling a half-peeled banana and trying to soothe him. When she caught sight of Autumn, wariness took the place of the stress stamped on her classical features.

"Oh! It's you. I'm not certain who the little guy is, but I've been trying to charm him for the last few hours. Initially, it worked, but I'm afraid he requires food and a nap."

Her accent was an odd combination of British and American, and her long black hair was swept back in a French braid. She also wore no makeup, but it didn't detract from her natural beauty or her peaches-and-cream complexion. Autumn experienced an odd vertigo from seeing her mother's clone.

"He dislikes bananas," Autumn replied inanely. A feeling of embarrassment began to take hold as she stared at Angelica Thorne. A good mother would've seen to her child first, but all Autumn could do was stare. Seeing this carbon copy of her mother was disconcerting.

"And he's made it bloody well known," Angelica replied with a weary grimace. "I'm not sure how you would know that, though, Autumn. Or why *you* of all people should care." Coldness crept into the other woman's tone, and oddly, it stung to be misjudged by a person whose twin she adored beyond measure.

"I'm not who you believe me to be. I'm—"

"Mama! Mama!" Jolly screamed, flailing his arms in her direction. "Mama!"

His cry broke the spell holding her in place. Rushing forward, Autumn scooped him into her arms, holding tight to his compact body and breathing in the scent of his sweaty hair.

"Hey, fry guy. Mama's here. Mama's here." Tears stung the back of her closed lids, and she silently vowed to do better. Swore to protect him from incidents like this in the future. "I'm sorry, Jolly. Mama's sorry you were lost."

"Who are you, if not Autumn Carlyle?" Angelica asked. Some of her icy disdain had disappeared, having been replaced by curiosity.

"Actually, I *am* Autumn Carlyle, but not from your

world. Right now, I don't have time to explain, but just know I brought LJ back to you."

"LJ?"

"She's been calling me that since we met, darlin'," he said as he approached. With a humorous glance in Autumn's direction, he grinned. "She said the flannel makes me look like a lumberjack."

"I had to call him something other than Alastair. It would've been too confusing otherwise."

"Why?" Angelica asked after kissing her husband's bearded jaw.

"Him." LJ gestured to Dapper Alastair, who stood about ten feet away, watching the scene with a fascinated expression. "The alternate-reality version of myself."

But Angelica's attention wasn't caught by Alastair, and instead, she was focused on the people beside him —Preston, Spring, Nash, and Aurora.

"Am I dreaming?" she asked.

"If you are, we are," Autumn said. She materialized a blanket and, with a wave of her hand, spread it beneath a large oak tree. After making herself comfortable, she held out her hand and conjured apple slices for Jolyon to eat. "Here you go, my sweet boy. This should take care of those hunger pangs."

Soon enough, he was happily munching away, alternating between bites and trying to shove the other half of the slice in Autumn's mouth. Playfully, she pretended to gobble his fingers. His giggles were music to her soul, and she prayed to the Goddess his time here hadn't scarred him. But that was a problem for another day.

"Uncle Alastair? Do you have Jolly's anklet?"

He knelt beside her and wordlessly handed her the finely crafted jewelry with the ability to temper Jolyon's formidable power. Autumn spared a moment to study the clasp, and after verifying it wasn't faulty, she grasped her son's wildly kicking leg.

"Steady now, munch. Mama's trying to put your pretty anklet back on."

Again, he kicked, and his heel connected with her forearm.

"The boy acts like he doesn't want you to put it on him," LJ said. "Could it be it bothers him?"

At a loss as to why it might, she faced Alastair. "Uncle Al?"

"Your guess is as good as mine, child. I'd say there was a reason either he or his sister tore it off, but until he's able to vocalize it or we find Chloe, we won't know for sure."

"May I?"

Spring held out her hand, and Autumn placed it in her palm. They all remained silent as she studied the piece. Autumn couldn't help but notice Angelica's fascination with Preston, nor it seemed, could LJ.

"Unbelievable, isn't it?" he said.

"Yes." With a small laugh, she shook her head. "To see him again after all this time, well, I can't seem to wrap my head around it. An alternate reality, you said?"

"Yep." Within a few minutes, she'd been brought up to speed on the day's events, and Autumn was talked out.

Her mother joined her on the blanket and pressed her back to the trunk. Using her arms to indicate Autumn should give her Jolly, she smiled when he dove into her embrace, and she accepted his sloppy kisses on her cheek like the indulgent grandmother she was.

"Thanks, Mama."

"You're welcome, darling girl." Taking one of Jolly's proffered apples, she rubbed her cheek against his downy head. "Why don't you take your father and go find Keaton and Chloe while I stay here with Jolly? Perhaps we'll get him down for a much-needed nap."

"If I've never told you this, you're the best." With a quick group hug that included her mother and son, Autumn rose. "Any idea which direction my husband went?"

"We thought he was coming to find you, but we reached you first," Alastair said with a frown. "I didn't see him on the journey here. Anyone else?"

They all shook their heads, giving Autumn cause for concern. What the hell had happened to her husband?

18

*A*utumn followed her instincts and headed for the Carlyle property. Reason suggested Chloe would look for the familiar, and Autumn only prayed she'd discover a kind soul to look out for her. How terrifying must it be for a young teen to find herself lost in an alternate dimension, misplace her toddler brother, and not be able to get help when she needed it?

Annoyed at the adults who should've known better, Autumn trudged through the woods. Grunts and what sounded like fists crunching bone hurried her steps, and she broke through a cove of trees to see her husband fighting another man.

"Mommy!"

Chloe's frantic shout brought her head around, and Autumn ran to scoop her into a tight embrace. Overcome, she blinked back the tears trying to crowd her eyes. "Oh, Chloe! I was so worried about you."

"I'm sorry," her daughter sobbed. "I'm so sorry, Mommy."

"None of that, kid." Drawing back, Autumn smoothed Chloe's tangled hair. "Your dad and I are just glad you're safe."

"But I lost Jolly, and—"

"We found Jolly, and he's fine. Promise."

Peering around, Chloe's brows drew together. "But he's not here."

"He's with my parents and Uncle Alastair. He's safe, too."

"They came?" she asked in disbelief. "Here? To this place?"

Surprised by Chloe's inability to understand why the others would come for her, Autumn knelt in front of her. "What's this all about? You know you're an honorary Thorne and our Witch Club president. Of course, everyone is going to look for you. We'd rip hell apart to get you back."

"Uh, Tums?"

Autumn lifted her gaze to Gothica.

"That's not your kid. *That* is Rachel."

Coldness invaded her face as the blood receded. The proof was in the little things: the texture of her hair and the smell of her shampooed head. Hell, even her body was skinnier. But the tipoff should've been that Chloe never called her "Mommy." It was always

"Mama." Yet Autumn had ignored the oddness of the word in her relief that her child was safe.

Feeling faint, she looked into the smug, dark eyes of the girl before her. How had she been able to fool her? Autumn could see through most people's bullshit in an instant.

Fury almost blinded her, and she gripped the girl's shoulders, giving her a hard shake. "Where's my kid?"

"I'm your kid, Mommy. I'm Chloe," Rachel lied.

"No, you're not. Whatever game you're playing, it needs to stop. Right now!"

The sounds of the dual-Keaton scuffle died away as Autumn's husband straightened and wiped the back of his wrist across his mouth, accidentally smearing his blood across his cheek instead of getting rid of it.

"What the fuck is going on? Of course that's Chloe," he panted out.

"No, Keat. It's not. When have you ever known her to use the word mommy?" With her finger and thumb, she tilted the girl's chin up. The small scar Chloe had received from a bicycle crash was missing from beneath. "I'll give you one opportunity to tell me where my daughter is, kid. Then I'm going to let my temper fly. Trust me, no one likes it when that happens."

Her tone was rigid, and her expression unyielding. Likely for the first time in Young Rachel's life, she'd met her match.

"She's in the shed," the girl said, giving off an

uncaring vibe. But Autumn saw deeper and recognized the blasé attitude for what it was. Loneliness and a sense of feeling unloved.

She ran her knuckles along the girl's soft cheek and smiled her gratitude. "Thank you, Rachel. Before you show me where it is, I want you to make nice and apologize to your aunt for the pranks you've pulled in the past."

Resentment flared to life on her face.

"This isn't a request, kid. Along with LJ, she's the only stable influence I've seen in this hellhole." Leaning in, Autumn met Rachel's gaze squarely. "She'll love you if you let her."

Moisture welled in the dark eyes staring back at her, and after a few rapid blinks, the girl looked up at Gothica. "Really?" she asked hoarsely.

After studying Rachel for an extraordinarily long moment, Gothica nodded. "I'd like that, if you would."

"You'll stay away from my daughter, darklin'!" Redneck Keaton shouted as he climbed to his feet. "She ain't gonna be like you and your kind!"

Rising, Autumn shot him a quelling glance and tucked Rachel into her side. "Shut the fuck up, asshole. You don't know what the hell you're saying."

"I don't care if you look like my slut wife or not. I'll not have you talk to me that way," he growled.

"She'll talk to you as she sees fit," Keaton snapped. "Spring has been nothing but helpful to us since we arrived, unlike you, ya dick." With a shove to the guy's chest, Keaton gave him a disgusted look. "If you weren't a lazy lush, your daughter might not be running unchecked through life. She might achieve something great."

"I want to be great," Rachel said softly.

The arrested expression on RK's face as he turned his attention to his daughter was encouraging, and Autumn prayed to the Goddess the man would wake up soon and realize the treasure he had.

With a probing stare at Gothica, he slowly nodded. "You can teach her the magic her ma won't?"

"I can," she replied.

"None of that black magic, voodoo shit, though," he warned.

"None of that. Just how to be a proper witch. Something my sister should've taught us both."

"Alright, then."

Autumn couldn't help wondering if her own counterpart here in this world had caused most of the problems for this father-and-daughter duo. If so, she definitely needed a swift kick to the ass. "Where's the shed?"

"'Bout a hundred yards that way." He gestured with his thumb toward the area that would contain the barn in Autumn's reality.

Signaling Keaton with a nod toward RK, she gripped Rachel's hand and stormed in the direction indicated. Rachel ran to keep up, but didn't complain. Behind them, Autumn could hear RK grumble as

Keaton not-so-nicely encouraged him to follow their small trio.

Gothica remained quiet until they had reached the edge of the property. "Wait, Tums. Let him go first. In case he's got traps in place."

"RK, get your butt moving," Autumn called back.

"RK?" he asked.

"Redneck Keaton."

For the second time since they met, Gothica's laughter was unrestrained. "I think I adore you," she gasped out.

"What's not to adore?" Autumn quipped as Rachel watched them in wide-eyed wonder.

"I wish my mom were like you," the girl suddenly whispered. "You're cool."

"Your mom and I will have a come-to-Jesus meeting before I go, kid. I promise you that."

19

Chloe's appearance was bedraggled and filthy, enraging Keaton and making him see red. Not as prone to forgiveness as his wife, he glared at Rachel before stepping into the shed and hauling Chloe up into his arms.

Like her clone had before, she sobbed, but hers wasn't an act. He cursed himself for being taken in by Rachel earlier. He now understood Goth Spring's response in sending Chloe away. If Rachel always gave such Oscar-worthy performances, it would be difficult to believe her. Ever.

Spouting assurances that she was safe, he rocked Chloe in his arms and fought a battle against his own sobs. Her heartbreak was his. Autumn joined him, wrapping her arms around them and tucking her head against Chloe's back.

"I'm sorry we didn't find you sooner, Chloe," she said achingly. "So sorry. But we're here now."

Lifting her head, Chloe nodded. "I knew you'd come, Mama. I knew."

"And I always will."

"I know that, too," their daughter said with a watery smile. Just as quickly, she sobered again and asked, "Did you find Jolly?"

"We did. He's with my parents and Uncle Alastair."

Relief caused Chloe's shoulders to drop, and she asked to be put down after she gave Keaton one more hard squeeze. "Will you take me to him? I want to see him."

"Yes, midge. We'll go there now." Taking her hand, he locked gazes with Autumn. "Where did you leave Jolly?"

"By the old oak with Winnie's and Zane's initials."

"But—"

She waved a hand in dismissal. "Yeah, I know there's no mark on the trunk itself, but it's in the same location."

"Gotcha." He bussed her forehead and gave her a significant look. He understood without words that she intended to find the other Autumn and read her the riot act for her negligence of Rachel. "You going to be okay here?"

"I will. I can't say it won't come to blows when I see my clone, though," she said with a grin. "That bitch deserves whatever she has coming."

"That's my vicious darling! Take no prisoners, babe." He returned her grin with one of his own. "I'll be back as soon as I deliver Chloe to Knox and your family."

"See you—"

The sunlit sky around them darkened to night, lightened, then darkened again.

"What the—" Redneck Keaton's exclamation was aborted as the world around them continually flickered from day to night.

"What is happening right now?" Autumn muttered.

Static electricity hung heavily in the air and sounded like the popular rice cereal with its snap, crackle, and pop once milk was added to the bowl.

"It's the Goddess trying to break through," Gothica Spring told them. "Periodically, she tries, but she's been cut off for years."

"You can't summon the Goddess?" Keaton asked incredulously. "Like, *ever*?"

She shook her head in response. "I've never seen it this intense before. She must *really* want to come through."

Lightning struck an outcrop of rocks about nine yards from where they stood, causing Chloe and Rachel to scream. Keaton's nerves were fried in the process, making him jumpy and eager to avoid another display of supernatural power. He drew his daughter and Rachel closer to him and shot the Thorne women a worried glance.

"I'm not a fan of the fireworks, and neither are the girls."

"I say we give the Goddess help," Autumn replied with a thoughtful look at the blackened boulders. "Gothica? Any ideas on how we can manage it?"

"Not really."

"My wife'll know," Redneck Keaton said softly, his eyes still locked on the strike zone. "Her family's the one who sealed off the deities' abilities to come here."

"What?" Unsure if he'd heard correctly or was in a bizzaro dream, Keaton shook his head. "Seriously, man. I think you need to repeat what you said. If it's what I think it is, we're going to need an explanation."

The other guy focused his attention on Spring. "You were the reason, girl. When you called on the dark arts, the gods wanted to strip you of your magic. Autumn was adamant that wasn't going to happen."

"You're blaming this on *me?"* Gothica's expression was pure outrage. "I didn't ask her to do that. I didn't even know she did."

"Thornes protect their own. *That*, you should know, or you would if you'd ever hung around."

The guy didn't sound happy about the fact, and Keaton shared a look with his wife. In her golden-amber eyes, he could see she didn't love this conversation, either.

Pasting on a determined expression, she approached Keaton's unkempt clone. "RK—"

"Stop calling me RK, woman! My name's Keaton."

"RK is fitting. *Redneck* Keaton," Gothica stressed not so helpfully.

Other than a red face and a slight downturn of his mouth, RK didn't react. Seemed the man had a healthy respect for the Thornes and what they could do.

"I'm sorry, Keaton," Autumn said softly to RK. "In my mind, it's the best way to tell you apart. Also, I suggest you get rid of the wife-beater shirts if you want to be taken seriously."

He surprised them when he laughed. "At least I wasn't dubbed PK."

Keaton knew he was a fool for asking. "PK?"

"Puss"—the man glanced at the girls as if registering their presence for the first time—"Uh, Prissy Keaton."

"This Priss just kicked your ass, so I'd be careful," Keaton warned in a growly voice.

"You got lucky. I'm sober now."

"Not hardly."

"Enough," Autumn snapped. "Tell us where to find the reversal spell your wife used. We need to set this place to rights."

20

In the end, they didn't need to, and the person who burst through the veil wasn't the Goddess at all, but a super-pumped steroid version of Knox Carlyle in Grecian garb.

"Holy sweet baby Jesus! It's Knox! In a toga!" Autumn exclaimed, unashamedly admiring the man's impressive bare chest.

Keaton was less than happy about her excitement. "Babe. Seriously?"

"It's not like I'm partaking in that particular beefcake," she replied with a laugh. "But just because I'm on a diet, it doesn't mean I can't admire what's in the pastry case."

Her husband's eye roll was accompanied by Gothica's girlish laugh. The delightful sound caught Half-Naked Knox's notice, and his interested gaze swept the length of Spring's hideously clad body. It was as if he could see underneath her awful clothing, because his steady-eyed stare grew hot and he strode toward her, looking like he wanted to eat *her* up.

Autumn stepped in front of him right before he took action. She was afraid he'd scoop Gothica up, toss her over his shoulder, and disappear into the woods for a little slap and tickle.

"Simmer down, big guy," she told him.

Gothica shoved her aside and stepped forward, wonder on her made-up face as he wrapped a large hand around the woman's neck, hauled her close, and disappeared before Autumn could blink.

"Well, that didn't go as planned," she muttered. "But I can't say I didn't see it coming."

"Does that mean he broke alternate-you's spell?" Keaton asked, clasping Chloe's hand and casting one last glance toward the now-blue sky.

"Not our problem to deal with. We need to get back to the others and figure out how to get home."

"Hopefully, our Spring will have the spell memorized."

Autumn prayed he was right. Before leaving, she paused before Rachel.

"She'll be back. Give her time to get her new beau out of her system, and she'll train you to be a witch."

Although the girl appeared skeptical, she nodded. Addressing Chloe, she said, "I'm sorry I locked you in the shed and stole your clothes."

"Why did you do it?" Chloe asked.

Rachel's dark gaze dropped to her toes, and she gave a half-hearted shrug. "I thought maybe Aunt Spring would believe I was you. Maybe everyone would, if they found out you came through today."

"What would that have gained you, Rachel?" Keaton asked gently.

"People who care," the girl whispered, and the sound of her loneliness was hard to hear.

Autumn pinned RK with a narrow-eyed stare. "Do better, asshole."

But he ignored her in favor of watching Keaton cover Chloe's shoulders with his large hands and squeeze lightly. Then, RK approached his daughter.

"I'm sorry, Rach. Sorry for being a shit daddy."

Surprise kept the girl silent.

He stroked trembling fingers down her dark hair and tentatively smiled. "If you can forgive me, maybe we can start fresh and I can do better, like our new friends suggested. Whatcha think?"

Nodding, she reached for his hand, but he bypassed her gesture to hug her.

"I love ya, Rach. I know I never tell you, but I do."

"What about Mama?"

RK winced. "Yeah, one thing at a time, alright?"

"Yeah."

"Okay, so I hate to destroy a tender moment, but we have to go. The longer we're here, the more the balance goes bye-bye," Autumn said. Giving in to instinct, she hugged Rachel. "Take care, kid. Stop being a brat, and seek out Alastair and Spring. They'll see you're taken care of and taught what you need to know. Got it?"

"Thank you, Mom—uh, Miss Autumn."

With a quicksilver smile for the father-daughter duo, she clasped Chloe's other hand and headed for the woods. They stopped a few yards away.

"Oh, RK?" Autumn called back.

"Yeah?"

"Tell your wife I said knock off her shit, or I'll find a way to come back and do it for her." She met his tired and dull eyes. "Your kid deserves a mom who's present, Keat. Don't either of you settle for less."

He smiled, and in his bloated face, she saw the ghost of her husband. "I'll remember."

"Good." With a nod toward the woods, she asked, "Any booby traps I need to be aware of?"

"Nah. We spread rumors so the locals leave us alone."

Laughing, she allowed her husband and daughter to lead her away.

"Think they'll patch things up?" Keaton asked her when it was just the three of them.

"Who knows? Clearly, my alternate-reality twin is an unfeeling bitch. It's easy to see he's hurting, and not just from the ass-kicking you gave him. I'm sad for them all."

"Me, too."

Chloe squeezed her hand. "I'm glad I got the good mom and dad."

"You did get pretty lucky, didn't you?" Keaton shifted to wrap an arm around Chloe's neck and drag her close. "Just like us."

"Just like us," Autumn repeated. "Let's go get Jolly."

21

*A*utumn's family was in the clearing, being guarded by the mammoth Cerberus, whose drool—while disgusting—no longer ate through everything it touched. The beast was taking special care to watch over her returned pup, that seemed fascinated with LJ.

Pausing, she held Keaton and Chloe back to watch the scene.

Startled, he glanced at her, then followed her sight line to the others. He, too, seemed able to appreciate the uniqueness of the crowd deep in discussion. The fact that there were practically two of everyone was discombobulating and gave the illusion of double vision, if one didn't look close enough to see their appearances were slightly altered by things like hair length and clothing.

"I love them."

Turning to face her, Keaton grinned. "I know you do, babe."

"No. I really fucking love them." She met his gaze and snorted softly. "I'm the hard-ass. The tough one of the group. The one everyone relies on to kick ass and take names later."

He nodded, a question in his clear blue eyes.

"But I think I love too much. Too hard."

"Why is that a bad thing?"

"It makes me reactive. Look at me, coming here, punching Gothica in the face, and tearing the world apart to find my kids."

His wide smile was engaging, and nothing but respect shone back at her from his gaze. "Babe, those are your superpowers. Not things to be ashamed of."

Chloe was watching her with a curious expression, as if waiting to see how this conversation would turn out.

"What do you think, kid?" she asked her daughter.

"I think you're the best mom ever." The raw honesty was visible for everyone to see and matched the awe in Chloe's voice. "I love you."

The rush of tears burned, and Autumn rapidly blinked them away as she bent and pulled Chloe into a bear hug. "I love you, too."

"And because you love so hard and too much, I know she'll always be protected if anything happens to me," Keaton said gruffly. The emotion of the moment got to him the same as them, and they spared a moment for a group hug.

"Let's go home." Autumn smiled down at Chloe and caressed her cheek. "Then we'll discuss what kind of puppy to get you and your brother. But only after you've been suitably grounded for practicing magic without an adult present."

"Aw, Mama!" But Chloe's complaint was half-hearted, and the idea of a new puppy brought forth her endearing grin. "Do I get to pick what kind?"

"We'll see. Certainly not a three-headed Cerberus."

In minutes, they'd joined their family from both sides of the portal. After the hugs and thank yous were spread around, their group linked hands.

"Spring?" Autumn looked to her younger sister for guidance to return to their reality.

"I'm—Oh!" Eyes wide, she stared at something beyond Autumn's shoulder. "Wow."

"Without turning, I can tell you caught sight of Half-Naked Knox," Autumn said dryly. "I had a similar reaction."

"One we're going to discuss when we are safely home," Keaton promised.

"Shhh. This feels like a weird dream anyway. Let me enjoy it."

His chuckle made her grin.

Knowing it would be a minute before they got their return spell sorted, Autumn dropped her husband's hand and twisted to see Gothica and HN

Knox approaching. They both looked rumpled and extremely satiated.

Autumn nodded her approval. "Good for her! Well done, Gothica!" she called out.

Goth Spring's flushed face was a joy to see. Perhaps she'd found the love she was denied by her selfish family.

"Now, I need you to get rid of your sexual brain fog and work with us to get home."

Grecian-clad Knox stepped forward, and Autumn noticed he didn't let go of Gothica's hand. Undoubtedly, the man was smitten.

"I can take care of that," he said. "All those planning to go through the portal, to the left. The others, stand on the right."

"What about the trade? How do we know whatever went through will return here?" Autumn asked.

"I'll make sure of it on this side, as Isis will on your side," he assured her.

Gothica sighed her adoration.

"He must've been something in bed to put that look on her face," Spring whispered in an aside.

Her Knox cleared his throat.

"I didn't say *you* weren't." Grin pert, she patted his chest, pausing to appreciate his muscles. "Clearly, some things are universal."

He laughed, drawing the attention of his godlike counterpart.

The two men studied each other with marked

interest before HN Knox spoke. "I can see your power radiating from you. Why haven't you taken your position with the deities?"

"Her." Tilting his blond head toward Spring, Knox smiled. "I go where she goes."

HN Knox studied Autumn's perfectly groomed sister before glancing down at Gothica and grinning. "I can understand why. I believe I've found my life's mission."

"Jesus, my heart just melted in my chest," Autumn quipped. "Okay, enough of the sap. My son needs to get home for his afternoon nap, or we're all going to be in trouble." Facing Alastair, she said, "Which reminds me, Uncle, we need to contact Isis to reattach that anklet."

"Prepare yourselves," HN Knox said.

The lights went out, and the pitch black was as disturbing the second time as it had been the first.

When their world righted itself, they were in the clearing, alone, and the rip in the fabric of space was sealing itself. Autumn saw the Cerberus puppies bounding toward their mother in the tiny slit of the opening. A second later, the space where she was staring looked like an open field framed by forest.

"I'm not going to believe this wasn't a dream," she muttered to herself. Turning to the others, she said, "Okay, head count."

EPILOGUE

"Chloe's missing!"

Autumn froze in her tracks to stare at Keaton.

Ten years had passed since their children had accidentally opened a portal to another world, and still, whenever she came home and found her husband in a tizzy because he couldn't find one of them or the other, she had a heart-stopping moment. But reason usually reasserted itself, and she would remember nothing could be as bad as that day so long ago. Chloe was now a young woman, and the likelihood was that she'd gone off with friends and hadn't opened an ancient book to conjure a three-headed hellhound.

Autumn's hands only shook a little when she set her shopping bags on the counter. "Missing how?"

"She should've been home a half hour ago. It's *her* birthday party." Keaton absently kissed her cheek, then went to the kitchen slider to stare out the back door as if seeking Chloe.

Joining him, Autumn looked at the newly gathered crowd on the pool deck.

"They're early," she muttered.

Keaton snorted. "No. You're just late."

After giving him a grimace and a side-eyed glare because she couldn't argue when he was one-hundred-percent correct, she let her gaze roam over their guests.

Spring was laughing with her husband, Knox, who held their five-year-old daughter, Megan, on his lap. The girl was petite, with large jade-green eyes, a riot of chestnut curls, and a sweet smile that was mainly reserved for her dad. It had to be hard for a shy child in a clan of loudmouths, but the girl never complained. Other than her unfortunate klutzy tendencies, she reminded Autumn of Spring at that same age. The intelligence in her watchful gaze couldn't be mistaken for anything but a big brain absorbing everything.

Across from the trio, Summer held Spring's son, Phillip, who at two was already the pint-sized image of his gorgeous father. With dancing blue eyes and a winning grin, the toddler was already learning to use his charm for evil. He was a particular favorite of the Goddess Serqet, who visited with regular frequency since she'd buried her centuries-old grudge against the couple. In her eyes, the little gremlin could do no wrong. In anybody's eyes, really. Only Knox was able to keep him in check. But Phillip did have a healthy respect for Alastair when he raised a brow in warning.

Winnie's triplets were in the pool, and being the terrorists they were, they splashed Olivia and Jolyon, who had their heads bent and were clearly conspiring against the trio of fourteen-year-old boys. Autumn knew this because it was always an all-out water war when the five of them were together in the pool. Yes, it was three against two, but Jolly and Ollie were a formidable duo when they teamed up, and they *always* teamed up.

Glancing away, Autumn scanned the deck, taking in the groupings of family and friends. She laughed when she spotted Alastair in a loose flannel button-up over top of his pale-blue tee-shirt. It was a cool spring afternoon, but weather was nothing to witches able to control their body temperatures. Ever since their trip through the portal, he'd dress down for family functions like this.

Moving on, she did a head count. Everyone was there, and everything was set up for the birthday girl, who appeared MIA.

"Have you tried scrying for her? Or have you messaged Damian to see if she's there?" she asked Keaton.

"You know I only seek the Aether as a last resort. I'd never admit this to anyone else, but that guy scares the shit out of me."

Autumn held out her hand, earning a look of confusion from Keaton.

Grinning, she wiggled her fingers. "Your man card. Hand it over."

"Rude."

"Only a little," she agreed as she stepped into his arms and curled hers around his neck. "The house is empty—"

"Except for our other monster, who is standing right behind you."

Dipping his head, Keaton kissed her. It wasn't as long or as amorous as Autumn preferred, but it was enough to tide her over until they could find alone time. She released him to welcome their youngest son, William.

Dutifully, he lifted his face so she could give him butterfly kisses with her nose.

"How's the sweetest little warlock on the planet? Hmm?"

His amber eyes sparkled even as he groaned. "Mom! You can't say those things anymore. Everyone thinks I'm a baby."

"You're *my* baby."

"I'm ten. Practically grown up."

"Pfft. You're nowhere *near* grown up, and besides, you'll always be my baby, Will."

He grinned, and she was forgiven for treating him like a small child. Heaving an internal sigh, she reminded herself to give him his wings. With his auburn hair, golden eyes, and hair-trigger temper, William was her kid all the way. But he also knew how to laugh at himself and have fun. Those traits, he'd inherited from Keaton.

"Do you happen to know where Chloe went?" she asked as she began unloading the last-minute grocery items onto the counter. Soda, various-flavor potato chips, and Cheetos were a required party staple for the next generation and the one thing she refused to conjure. She'd be damned if she would use her power to feed their junk-food addictions.

When he reached for the bag of barbecue chips, she tapped his hand and pointed to the cabinet. "Bowl!"

"Chloe's with Sabrina and Aeden. Something having to do with her upcoming finals."

"I suppose we should've planned the party for after," Keaton said, ripping open the Cheetos bag and ignoring Autumn's glare.

William, smart boy he was, returned to the kitchen island with four large bowls and handed one to his dad.

"Bowl. And don't sneak anything to the dog," he told him, much to Autumn's and Keaton's amusement. William was a fifty-year-old in a child's body.

Pausing her sorting action, she turned to face him and put a hand on her hip. "Did she say when she was going to return?"

His reply was the standard one-shoulder Thorne shrug.

"Great. Just great," she muttered.

"No one cares, Mom." Will stretched to kiss her cheek, then tucked four of the two-liter soda bottles in his arms and headed for the door. "They just like hanging out," he said over his shoulder.

Keaton continued to stuff his face as she emptied the food into bowls.

"He's right, ya know," he said. "Our family would get together whether there was a special occasion or not. They appreciate the bond and the routine."

"I know, but I wanted to make this special for her. She's graduating in another couple of months and will be going off on her own."

"I know, babe. Trust me. It's a lot harder for me to let her go than for you."

Autumn removed the bag from his hands and replaced it with the filled dishes. "Yeah. Talk about an overbearing father."

His grin flashed, telling her he wasn't offended, but it quickly died. "Have you noticed anything strange about her lately? Beyond the average twenty-two-year-old wanting to move out and conquer the world."

"Yes. And I suspect it has to do with Derek. She's upset that he's got himself a new girlfriend." Autumn met his steady stare and grimaced. "Deep in her heart, she loves him. Always has since they were kids and he saved her from Zhu Lin."

Keaton nodded. "But because he's a few years

older, he's a man of the world and not ready to settle down with a childhood friend. Am I close?"

"Yes. She's hurting, and I think she needs to hide from those closest to her for a bit."

"So they don't see her pain," he concluded.

"So they don't see her pain," she agreed.

"Still, I'm going to text her again. She needs to make an appearance."

"She'll answer for me. Take this tray outside for the kids, and I'll call her."

After a check of their surroundings, he stepped up to her and wrapped an arm around her waist. "We can let the others wait a while longer, and I can welcome you home properly now."

His suggestive tone set her afire, and for one brief second, she considered a quickie. But their family members were all outside, expecting a birthday party.

"Hold that thought until tonight, babe." She ran her hand down the front of his shorts and rubbed, grinning when she felt his immediate response. "And be sure you're well rested."

"Dammit, woman! Now you'll have to serve the food. I've got an erection to kill."

With a girly giggle, she picked up the tray. "Fine. But then you'll be the one responsible for getting Chloe's ass here. She's got a party to attend. Use my phone and tell her I said boys are dumb and not worth losing sleep over."

"Hey!"

One of her brows shot up, and he gave her a sheepish look in return.

"Fine. We're a dumb lot."

"I didn't say *men* were dumb, just boys. You've gotten smarter with age."

His bark of laughter made her heart happy.

"I adore you, babe. You know that, right?" she asked him.

"Yeah. The feeling's mutual."

The warmth in his eyes was a welcome sight. They would never be like their alternate versions. They'd never go down the wrong path. And, even if they somehow did, they'd find their way back to each other, like they'd done sixteen years before. Theirs was a solid, forever kind of love.

Boundless.

Autumn had all she'd ever dreamed of and more.

FROM THE AUTHOR

Thank you for taking the time to read **Boundless Magic**! *I hope you enjoyed reading Autumn and Keaton's follow-up story as much as I enjoyed writing it. Please consider leaving a review if you're of a mind to. I'd greatly appreciate it.*

While there are currently no more stories in The Thorne Witches: HEAs series, there are two more paranormal romance series coming your way in addition to book #14 in the original Thorne Witches series. Be sure to preorder your copy of **Captivating Magic** *today!*

Be sure to subscribe to my mailing list to learn about new releases.

For fans who like to interact, my Facebook group entitles readers to "fan only" contests, as well as an exclusive first look at covers, excerpts and more. **Cromer's Carousers** *is the most fun way to follow yet. Keep turning to the last page for the links. I hope to see you there!*

Love & Lemon Drops,
T.M. Cromer
www.tmcromer.com

TURN THE PAGE FOR A LIST OF MY STORIES!

BOOKS BY T.M. CROMER

Get your printable list here:
www.tmcromer.com/printable-booklist

PARANORMAL ROMANCE

The Sentinels of Magic Series:
THE AETHER
THE DEATH DEALER
THE SEER

The Unlucky Charms Series:
PINTS & POTIONS
WHISKEY & WITCHES
BEER & BROOMSTICKS
COCKTAILS & CAULDRONS
WINE & WARLOCKS
HIGHBALLS & HEXES

The Thorne Witches Series:
SUMMER MAGIC
AUTUMN MAGIC
WINTER MAGIC
SPRING MAGIC

REKINDLED MAGIC
LONG LOST MAGIC
FOREVER MAGIC
ESSENTIAL MAGIC
MOONLIT MAGIC
ENCHANTED MAGIC
CELESTIAL MAGIC
EVERLASTING MAGIC
CAPTIVATING MAGIC

The Thorne Witches: Happily Ever Afters Series:
ENDURING MAGIC
BOUNDLESS MAGIC

The Angels of Legend Series:
LUCIFER
GABRIEL

CONTEMPORARY & ROMANTIC SUSPENSE

The Fiore Vineyard Series:
PICTURE THIS
RETURN HOME
ONE WISH

The Holt Family Series:
GOODBYE TO YOU

THIS TIME YOU

INCLUDING YOU

A LIFE WITH YOU

The Stonebrooke Series:

BURNING RESOLUTION

HIDDEN RESOLUTION

TURN THE PAGE FOR A LIST OF MY SOCIAL MEDIA LINKS!

BIO & FOLLOW LINKS

T.M. Cromer is a multi-award-winning, international best-selling author, who loves to craft wildly entertaining stories designed to keep you glued to your seat, turning the pages to find out what the hell happens next. She specializes in kickass heroines and the men who adore them.

Genres she writes include paranormal romance and romantic suspense.

Want to stay up to date on what's happening in the world of T.M. Cromer? Subscribe to her newsletter at https://www.tmcromer.com/newsletter or text JOIN to 1-877-795-1526 to receive release news and promo alerts.

You can also join her VIP reader group on Facebook to chat with her, participate in polls, or just keep current on what's happening. Become a member today at http://www.facebook.com/groups/cromer-scarousers.

FOLLOW T.M. CROMER:

- facebook.com/tmcromer
- instagram.com/tmcromer
- tiktok.com/@tmcromer
- bookbub.com/authors/t-m-cromer
- pinterest.com/tmcromer
- amazon.com/stores/T.M.-Cromer/author/B011QK3WXY

Milton Keynes UK
Ingram Content Group UK Ltd.
UKHW020646080324
439098UK00013B/385